Praise for *At the End of the Road*

"Unsettling suspense and chilling tone . . . A disturbing (in a good way) coming-of-age story with one of the creepiest characters to inhabit my imagination in a while—a paralyzed man with 'a distinctively reptilian appearance' who might be the devil on Eden Road." —*Milwaukee Journal Sentinel*

"Irresistibly creepy . . . Reminiscent of classic thrillers . . . from *Psycho* to *Deliverance*, *Whatever Happened to Baby Jane* to *Nightmare on Elm Street*, and not since *Lord of the Flies* have we seen children at the mercy of such meanness from their own kind." —*The Atlanta Journal-Constitution*

"Absolutely pitch-perfect . . . Deserving of a place on shelves alongside the all-time classic coming-of-age stories ever written." —*The Florida Times-Union*

Praise for *A Very Simple Crime*

"*A Very Simple Crime* is the product of A Very Talented Writer. Grant Jerkins's stylish prose and rich characters set him apart. As a reader, you will enjoy every page. It's impossible this is a first novel. Don't miss it." —Ridley Pearson, *New York Times* bestselling author of *In Harm's Way*

"The degree of wickedness in [Jerkins's] stylish legal thriller still delivers a chill . . . There's not a soul you can trust in the story . . . [A] well-fashioned but extremely nasty study in abnormal psychology, which dares us to solve a mystery in which none of the normal character cues can be taken at face value." —*The New York Times Book Review*

continued . . .

"A masterfully Hitchcockian story . . . Every time you think you know where things are headed and what a character is about, Jerkins throws in another twist that leaves you shaking your head at its diabolical cleverness. This is not, however, a book for the faint of heart . . . Jerkins's writing is both brilliant and brutal . . . Endlessly fascinating. *A Very Simple Crime* is a very impressive debut. Grant Jerkins has serious skills, and you'll be kicking yourself if you don't jump on board his bandwagon and get a comfy seat *now* because [it's] going to be standing room only soon."   —*Savannah Morning News*

"Gritty, sordid, disturbing, and addictive."
—*Richmond Times-Dispatch*

"So stylishly twisted that I read it in one sitting."
—*Milwaukee Journal Sentinel* (Top 10 List)

"No one in this novel is as they appear to be, and the twists and turns never let up until the very last page. This dark, chilling debut . . . is a real page-turner and should especially appeal to legal thriller fans."   —*Library Journal* (starred review)

"You have to admire the purity of Jerkins's writing: He's determined to peer into the darkness and tell us exactly what he sees."
—*The Washington Post*

"Beautifully plotted . . . Wholly original, funny, scary, haunting . . . and oddly arresting from the very first sentence."
—Nicholas Kazan, playwright and Oscar-nominated screenwriter of *Reversal of Fortune*

"Jerkins juggles his plot twists like a top circus acrobat in this nasty legal noir."   —*Publishers Weekly*

Berkley Prime Crime titles by Grant Jerkins

A VERY SIMPLE CRIME

AT THE END OF THE ROAD

THE NINTH STEP

THE NINTH STEP

GRANT JERKINS

BERKLEY PRIME CRIME, NEW YORK

THE BERKLEY PUBLISHING GROUP
Published by the Penguin Group
Penguin Group (USA) Inc.
375 Hudson Street, New York, New York 10014, USA
Penguin Group (Canada), 90 Eglinton Avenue East, Suite 700, Toronto, Ontario M4P 2Y3, Canada
(a division of Pearson Penguin Canada Inc.) • Penguin Books Ltd., 80 Strand, London WC2R 0RL,
England • Penguin Group Ireland, 25 St. Stephen's Green, Dublin 2, Ireland (a division of Penguin
Books Ltd.) • Penguin Group (Australia), 250 Camberwell Road, Camberwell, Victoria 3124, Australia
(a division of Pearson Australia Group Pty. Ltd.) • Penguin Books India Pvt. Ltd., 11 Community
Centre, Panchsheel Park, New Delhi—110 017, India • Penguin Group (NZ), 67 Apollo Drive,
Rosedale, Auckland 0632, New Zealand (a division of Pearson New Zealand Ltd.) • Penguin Books
(South Africa) (Pty.) Ltd., 24 Sturdee Avenue, Rosebank, Johannesburg 2196, South Africa

Penguin Books Ltd., Registered Offices: 80 Strand, London WC2R 0RL, England

This book is an original publication of The Berkley Publishing Group.

PUBLISHING HISTORY
Berkley Prime Crime trade paperback edition / September 2012

Library of Congress Cataloging-in-Publication Data

Jerkins, Grant.
The ninth step / Grant Jerkins.—1st ed.
p. cm.
ISBN 978-0-425-25598-8 (pbk.)
1. Life change events—Fiction. 2. Secrets—Fiction.
3. Self-realization in women—Fiction. 4. Psychological fiction. I. Title.
PS3610.E69N56 2012
813'.6—dc23
2012014770

PRINTED IN THE UNITED STATES OF AMERICA

10 9 8 7 6 5 4 3 2 1

For William Irish and John O'Brien

I would like to thank Robert Guinsler of Sterling Lord Literistic and Natalee Rosenstein of Berkley Prime Crime. Also at Berkley, my thanks to Robin Barletta, Megan Gerrity, Andromeda Macri, Kayleigh Clark, and Amy J. Schneider.

I'm grateful to Tricia Parks and Gary Mullet for checking my math. Any errors in that regard are mine alone.

Lots of friends—old and new—also helped out along the way. Readers and supporters include Carmen Tanner Slaughter, Becky Hann Kraegel, Renea Winchester, Robert Leland Taylor, Ed Schneider, Kris Stowers, Jan Thomas, Delphia Early Hudson, and Cathy Blanco. Sandy McGrew offered some insights into alcohol and tranquilizers. And my newest buddies, Ellen Schlossberg and retired Atlanta police sergeant Connie Locke, of Mt. Yonah Book Exchange, in Cleveland, Georgia, were of great assistance to me.

And always, Andria.

Chronic remorse, as all the moralists are agreed, is a most undesirable sentiment. If you have behaved badly, repent, make what amends you can and address yourself to the task of behaving better next time. On no account brood over your wrong-doing. Rolling in the muck is not the best way of getting clean.

—ALDOUS HUXLEY

1

GOTH WAS OVER

At two thirty in the afternoon, while teaching his last class of the day, ninth-grade geometry teacher Edgar Woolrich was thinking about the online auction that ended that night. The listing was for a vintage Japanese puzzle box—of which he, admittedly, already had many. But this particular box was special. It had five hidden compartments. Quite rare. The final price could easily climb into the thousands. Or, the obverse, a true bargain could be had.

Timing his bid would be critical. It was Friday night, so one could extrapolate that many potential bidders would be out at social functions. There were time zones to consider. Potential bidders on the West Coast could still be stuck in late-day commutes, while Edgar would be snug at home, his mouse pointer poised over the "confirm bid" button. Of course, ubiquitous handheld devices lessened that edge considerably. And the auction already had eighteen people watching it. Plus you had to factor in folks like Edgar himself who never clicked the "watch this item" button—lest they tip their hand in some unforeseen way.

No, the factoring that came into play while bidding on an online auction was like plotting irrational numbers on an infinite grid.

The lines of intersection were beyond reckoning, the variables endless.

"The triangle," Edgar said, "is God's own perfection."

Nobody heard him. While he had been daydreaming about the puzzle box, his class had taken advantage of his inattentiveness.

Edgar picked up the music triangle that he had borrowed from Mrs. Frazer, the band teacher, and struck it repeatedly with the metal wand. All of the students looked to the front, and the classroom grew quiet. Edgar wrapped his fingers over the vibrating metal instrument to stop the lingering note.

"Forget circles. The circle is the pursuit of madmen. If it's perfection you're after"—Edgar motioned to the triangle and dropped his voice into a pitch-perfect Al Pacino as Tony Montana—"Then say hello to my little friend." The kids laughed. Everybody loved *Scarface*. "This percussion triangle is equilateral. All sides equal. See? The angles too. Sixty degrees." He used his fingers to bridge the gap where one corner of the instrument didn't meet. "Now a right triangle like the one drawn on the board has a ninety-degree angle. See it? And God put one man on earth to figure out the perfection that is the right triangle. And that man's name was Pythagoras." Edgar glanced through the top half of his bifocals, looking into his students' faces, making sure he still had their attention. He did. "Now Pythagoras lived over two thousand years ago. And in this little town he lived in, he was really popular. With the girls. Right? Pythagoras was really popular with the girls because he had this really big . . . theorem." This got him some laughs, and he could see that all the class was watching him closely to see how far he'd take the joke. Edgar himself didn't know how far he'd take it. He'd been known to do some pretty bizarre stuff to get his point across to a room full of bored high school freshmen. And this was a remedial class, covering basics most students had mastered by seventh or eighth grade. These kids were almost genetically predisposed not to comprehend math. Sometimes shock and awe was the only method that worked. But these were PC times, and it seemed like every other week some suburban teacher ended up with his or her face displayed on the six o'clock news for inappropriate conduct and soon after tendered a "voluntary" resignation. And there you were, no more discretionary income for Japanese trick boxes. Not to mention food, clothing, and mortgage payments. No, soon you would be selling off your own puzzle boxes and applying for a food stamps EBT card.

Edgar paused to place the percussion triangle back in his briefcase so that he would be sure to remember to return it to Mrs. Frazer. While his attention was diverted, he heard titters of suppressed laughter from the back of the class, as well as a clear "ewwwww" of disgust. Edgar glanced up, his eyes automatically going to the spot from which trouble was most likely to come. Where it always came from. He peered through his thick bifocals at the pale skinny boy seated at desk seventeen. Martin Kosinski was so white and thin, the boy looked damn near skeletal. His face was furiously flushed with embarrassment, highlighting pimples like little red-topped volcanoes ready to erupt. Edgar could see that tears were threatening to overflow the boy's mascara-lined eyes.

Every year there was at least one of them. A natural-born target. This year it had been Martin. The kid was just so damn odd. The jet-black hair was quite clearly a dye job. And nobody's skin was that pale; it had to be powdered. Throw in the Johnny Cash wardrobe and the kid stood out like a whore in church. Edgar realized that high school was a time when children discovered and defined their adult identities, and that process was a rocky one for many of them. But Goth? Hell, even Edgar knew that Goth was over.

The predators were abundant. Always. There were plenty of bullies to go around. And, as always, there was the King Bully. The one who set the pace, who defined just how intense and cruel the torment would be. The crown this year went to Jack Mendelson, a fifteen-year-old with thick beard stubble, thick muscles, and a thick head.

So why not move Martin so that he wasn't sitting directly in front of King Bully? It had been Edgar's experience that a course of action such as that invariably failed. It was a step toward seclusion. It perpetuated rather than halted. Edgar had always sat the students alphabetically, and if he started switching them around midyear, it not only taught Martin that the solution to life's problems was evasion, but it also sent the message to Mendelson that he had won. And Edgar was adamant that Mendelson would not win. Not on Edgar's watch.

Although he hadn't actually seen him do anything, Edgar said by rote, "Jack Mendelson, hands to yourself. It's not a difficult concept. Thank you." Mendelson offered none of the protests of the wrongfully accused, so Edgar figured that he'd been right and moved on. "In fact, Pythagoras's theorem was so big that—"

Jason McNiel, the pimples on his forehead also looking Vesuvian, held his hands about a foot apart and asked, "This big?" The classroom exploded with laughter, and Edgar laughed right along with them. This was what he wanted.

"No. Bigger. His theorem was so big . . ." Edgar cupped his hand around his ear and leaned forward.

The class didn't disappoint and boomed in unison: "How big was it?"

"It was so big that virtually every other mathematical theorem advanced since has been influenced by—" From the corner of his eye, Edgar saw Martin twist forward in his desk with a jerky motion.

"Has been influenced by it. It's pretty simple actually." Although he knew the theorem by heart, Edgar leaned over his desk, head down, running his finger across an open page of the textbook, as though trying to locate some tidbit of information to impart.

"The Pythagorean theorem just says that in a right triangle, and I know you guys remember what a right triangle is. I just said it. That in a right triangle, the sum of the squares of the two legs coming off the right angle . . ." Edgar paused, leaning farther into the text, as if locating the exact wording. With his head tilted thus, Edgar created a sort of prism with his rimless glasses that allowed him a murky view of the classroom. He could see that Mendelson, all 220 pounds of him, was making a grand show of picking his nose. As best Edgar could tell, the kid mined a pretty good one and held it out proudly for the others to admire. Mendelson then leaned forward and carefully wiped the booger on Martin's pale neck.

Edgar slammed his book closed with a sharp crack. "Class, excuse me." He made a straight line for Mendelson and with his hand around the boy's meaty biceps, extracted him from his desk.

"Let's go."

"Dude, it's chaos. Mad fuckery."

"That, Mr. Mendelson, will cost you. Principal's office. Now."

2

GREAT PUMPKIN

At two thirty in the afternoon, Helen Patrice was having one of those days. For some reason, she just couldn't get the needle into the vein on the Great Dane's foreleg.

Her brown hair was pulled back with a simple elastic band, and Helen's eyes focused with sharp intent on the task at hand. Her vet tech, Elmore, was using every ounce of his considerable girth to hold the dog, Mitzi, still.

In a series of movements that she had performed countless times before, Helen extended Mitzi's foreleg and quickly found the main vein to the back of the leg. Although many vets now drew blood from the animal's jugular, as a leg draw was supposedly more painful for the dog, Helen didn't care for the risk of interstitial hemorrhage that went along with a jugular draw.

Elmore had Mitzi's head cradled firmly in the crook of his left arm. His right hand was clasped around the dog's upper leg, pulling the skin taut so that the vein was visible. Helen put her thumb on it and gently pressed, making the vein rise. But every time she tried to pierce it, the vein rolled. From deep inside, the Great Dane had started to growl a warning that she wasn't going to take much more of this sticking. "Poor baby," Helen cooed to the dog. "We'll get it this time. Promise."

Helen looked up at the Great Dane's owner, who had been silently observing the process. "Talk to her," Helen told the man. "Soothe her with your voice." The man cleared his throat but didn't speak.

At last, Helen felt the 21-gauge butterfly needle penetrate the vein and halted the forward motion as soon as she saw a flash of blood in the tubing, careful not to penetrate the posterior wall and blow the vein. She pushed the vacuum tube into the hub at the opposite end of the draw set and watched clean red blood spring into the thin surgical tubing and collect in the vial. "Got it." She kissed the Great Dane's cold wet nose. "Good girl, Mitzi." Elmore eased his grip on the dog but stayed close by.

Helen treated the blood sample with an anticlotting agent. She added formalin and placed the preparation in the centrifuge. Once the sample had spun down, Helen prepared a blood smear using an acid phosphate stain and placed the slide under the microscope to complete the microfilaria test. The whole process took about ten minutes. She hardly needed to look at the results. Leaning over the microscope, she found the point

of focus, and sure enough, there they were—the distinct serpentine squiggles of *Microfilariae*, heartworm larvae. One of the
larva was coiled in a triple loop and looked exactly like the snake
in the "Don't Tread on Me" flag.

Helen could feel the eyes of the dog's owner watching her.
He was a tall young man with a bulbous, pumpkin-like head.
He would have been otherwise ordinary looking except that his
lips were so thin that he appeared to simply have an opening in
his face: a mouth like a child might carve on a jack-o'-lantern.

Usually, Helen talked to and reassured the pet owners during test procedures, but Pumpkin Head had a nonchalant atti-
tude that frankly irritated Helen. He had come in saying that
the dog was listless, had no appetite, and had developed a constant cough. Last year he had "been talked into" paying twelve
hundred dollars to own a purebred harlequin Great Dane. And
that was a lot of money. And he really couldn't afford a vet bill,
but, at the same time, he couldn't see losing twelve hundred
bucks if the dog up and died. He had been thinking about breed-
ing the dog—and he always referred to her as "the dog," though
he had written *Mitzi* on the admittance paperwork—because
even if he sold the puppies at a grand each, that was solid money.

Helen thought that she would be hard pressed to imagine a
more distasteful recipe for animal cruelty than Pumpkin Head
going into the dog-breeding business.

Helen raised her head from the microscope and looked the
owner squarely in the eye. "I thought you said Mitzi was on
heartworm prevention."

"She is."

"And you give it every month?"

The man looked down at his shoes. "I try to. It's just hard to remember those things every single month."

Elmore and Helen shared a quick glance. Elmore arched his eyebrow.

"Yes," Helen said. "Well, I know what's causing her cough. Heartworms."

"Great. How much is that gonna cost?"

Helen closed her eyes and took a slow, steady breath. "Yes, luckily there is a treatment for this otherwise fatal disease." She snapped off her latex gloves and tossed them in the trash. "Treatment runs about nine hundred dollars."

The owner whistled through his slit of a mouth and appeared to give the matter some careful consideration. "How much to have her put to sleep?"

"Put her to sleep? Because you can't remember to give her a pill once a month?" Helen closed her eyes and pinched the bridge of her nose, trying to gather her thoughts and stem the anger she felt threatening to erupt in a less than professional manner. Elmore watched her closely, and when she opened her eyes again, he saw that they had turned to cold marble. Unconsciously, Elmore tightened his grip on the Great Dane.

Helen reached down and pulled the blood smear slide from the microscope and held it out to Mitzi's owner. "How about this, Great Pumpkin. How about as a helpful hint, I shove this slide up your ass? Think you could remember then?"

Pumpkin Head crossed the room and took his dog away

from Elmore. He hooked Mitzi's leash to her dog collar and headed for the door. Over his shoulder he said, "You just lost a customer, lady."

"Stop. Before I cry."

Elmore smiled.

3

THE BOY NEEDED SAVING

"I believe it's the correct thing," Edgar said. "What they want isn't to hurt you, it's to get you to react. And when you react, it just perpetuates the situation. It encourages further provocation. For every action, there is an equal and opposite reaction. But you can stymie the equation. Don't react."

"I'm not a coward," Martin said.

The classroom was empty except for the two of them.

"No, you're not a coward. To be a man, to grow, you have to sometimes suffer fools."

"So, when someone wipes a booger on my neck, I shouldn't do anything?"

The boy had a point. "Do what you're doing now. Talk to me." Even as he said it, Edgar knew that was pretty thin advice.

13

The boy needed saving, and it was Edgar's job to save him. "I can promise you that he won't be bothering you again. One more incident and Principal Cleage assures me that Jack Mendelson is going on an extended vacation. I give you my word." Edgar looked the boy over, started to reach out and touch him, but then decided against it. "And think about toning down some of this, this, uh . . . all this black."

Martin smiled. Almost.

4

SCHIZONUCLEOSIS

Sitting at the desk in her office, Helen signed off on the last chart of the day. Although she didn't think in such terms, Dr. Helen Patrice was living her life's dream. Yes, she sometimes had to deal with the Great Pumpkins of the world, but she also got to care for animals every day. And even though she had an SBA loan to pay on every month, and had used every cent of equity in her house to keep the business afloat, and some months had to pay the rent with her American Express card, she owned this veterinary practice. It was hers.

Helen opened the desk drawer and retrieved her purse. From the purse she pulled a mini bottle of Absolut vodka and broke the seal. Holding the chart up to shield her actions, Helen chugged the contents, put the empty bottle back in her purse, and popped an Altoid from the tin sitting on her desk. The whole process was quite fluid and took less than three seconds. Most of that time was spent in actually getting the vodka out of the bottle and into her mouth. The bottle was so small and the neck so tight, it felt like it took forever for the liquor to gurgle out, so Helen had taken to sucking it out in two quick draws. She did this three, perhaps four times during the course of each workday. Her office door stood open. She never closed it. And should one of her staff walk in during one of those critical three-second periods, all that could be seen was Dr. Patrice closely studying a chart.

By most anyone's definition of the word, Dr. Helen Patrice was an alcoholic, and had been since she took her first drink at the age of twelve. Helen was very much aware that she was what was commonly referred to as a functional alcoholic. She believed that she labored under no illusions on that particular score. She was an intelligent, well-educated woman. She knew who she was. For her, the crucial division of that term, that label, was not that she was an alcoholic. No, the critical aspect was that she was functional. She was doing just fine.

The drinking during the day was new—well, newish, anyway. It wasn't something she wanted to do. She didn't *desire* the drink. It was, in actuality, medicine.

Over the last year, the nature of her hangovers had changed. Despite ever-escalating quantities of booze, she'd never even had a rough morning after until she was in her twenties. Her memory of herself as a college student was that of a young woman who could drink all she liked without ever having to pay a physical price for it. But the alcohol abuse had started catching up with her around age twenty-five. Hangovers. Every day. But they were manageable. Something to be overcome each morning. A small obstacle. A fog to be burned off. A discomfort that could be remedied with plenty of fluids and healthy foods.

And remedy them she did. In fact, each day's recovery was celebrated with another night of drinking to the point of passing out, so that the next day, when the morning light came streaming in, she could, in the prophetic words of Jackson Browne, get up and do it again. Amen.

Say it again. Amen.

But now, at age thirty-five, she found that her hangovers bordered on a brand of mental illness. Whereas before she could easily sleep well past noon if given the chance, she now woke most mornings well before her alarm clock went off. There was no gradual, groggy ascent into wakefulness, but a startling crack of consciousness that overtook her each morning. Her mind raced with anxious thoughts of past wrongs, of dreaded diseases, of house fires waiting to erupt from faulty wiring. She saw herself as a badly scarred burn victim, a chemo-wracked cancer patient, a radiation-poisoned victim of a terrorist's dirty bomb. She imagined a brown recluse spider scurrying up her leg, picking the best place to bite her—practically feeling the agonizing burn of the venom going in, followed by the necrotic sear of rotting flesh. Everything bad. Everything bad that could happen or did happen. She saw it. All of it accompanied by a heart-racing sense of dread that felt borderline psychotic. And as hyper-driven as her mind was, her body was deathly sick, devoid of energy and seemingly unable to move. A soul-draining lethargy.

To her, all of this was like having schizophrenia and mononucleosis at the same time. It was schizonucleosis. That was what her hangovers had become. Schizonucleotic nightmares.

So, yes, the drinking was perhaps impeding her life more than it had in the past, but she was still managing. She was still functional. She had found a cure for schizonucleosis. It was as simple as taking another drink. Not drinking to get drunk, not even to catch a buzz—the real drinking was still reserved for her evenings. No, the daytime nips were just maintenance. An alleviation of her symptoms. When she omitted the maintenance drinks from her day, she was prone to tremors that made her job impossible. There were visual disturbances as well. Disturbances that bordered on the hallucinatory. So she drank herself better. Yes, it was bothersome, self-stigmatizing even, but, by God, she was *functional*.

If any other aspect of who she was bothered Helen on a conscious level, it was that she had in essence married the bottle. There were flings and brief romances, and, let's admit it, ugly little parking lot quickies that she didn't always entirely remember; but Helen Patrice was spoken for. She had her animals and her Absolut. And she had the cure. Life was good.

Kelly, a thick-bodied young woman who wore her makeup too heavy and who served as both the records clerk and receptionist, poked her head into Helen's office.

"Busy?"

"No, what's up?"

Kelly entered the office, trailing a dog on a leash behind her. "Elmore found this one wandering around the parking lot."

Helen sighed, not too terribly surprised to see Mitzi, the Great Dane. The dog was the size of a small pony. "Figures. Find her a spot in the kennel."

"Can't. Full."

"Then call the shelter."

"Did. Full."

Helen closed her eyes and pinched the bridge of her nose. "The Humane Society?"

When Helen opened her eyes again, Kelly silently mouthed the word *full.*

"Well," Helen said, "I'm not taking Marmaduke home."

"Well, neither am I."

"There's just no way in hell. She'll eat my cats."

Helen gently closed the hatchback on her tomato-red Honda Insight. Through the glass, Mitzi looked at her with eyes by Margaret Keane. The dog looked like a whale in a fishbowl.

Kelly and Elmore crossed the parking lot on the way to their cars. Kelly said, "We're going to Mulligan's tonight. Few drinks. Few dances. Interested?"

"No, not me. I've got Mitzi to contend with."

Elmore said, "Your problem is that you don't have a single redeeming vice."

Helen motioned to Mitzi. "That's my vice."

Elmore said, "Don't drink, don't smoke, what do you do?" Then he broke into dance and song, his large body moving with surprising grace.

Elmore twirled away, singing the old song, and Helen remembered that she needed to stop by the store on her way home and pick up a pack of cigarettes.

5

A TINY THING

Mantissa Cove was a good place to live.

On the way home, Edgar drove along the scenic highway that sketched the coastline. When he was anxious, the ocean always calmed him. And when he felt good, the ocean enhanced that feeling. Despite all evidence to the contrary, he felt there was something precise about the ocean.

On up the coast, sprawling onto the beach like an odd growth, was Pirate Land, a Coney Island–type amusement park. The roller coasters rose and fell in a way that reminded Edgar of curve graphs. It was closed, waiting for summer, and looked forlorn without people.

Past Pirate Land was a massive Greyhound bus terminal. It was the New England hub, and there was a sprawling parking

21

lot that held several hundred buses that had been sent here for maintenance, repairs, or to die. To Edgar, it was a sad place.

After the Greyhound terminal, Edgar turned onto Cove Boulevard, the main artery that led directly to Mantissa Cove's business district. From the business district, the boulevard quickly gave way to strip malls, fast food, and suburban sprawl. All of this in turn gave way to the older, more established neighborhoods on the outskirts of the town. The houses here enjoyed expansive yards that afforded lots of privacy. Banks of trees and long rows of overgrown hedges were abundant. This was where Edgar lived.

He and Judy had installed an inground swimming pool in their large backyard three years ago. They had enjoyed it a great deal in the beginning, but now it was just another burden, a chore to maintain, an impulse buy on which they were still making payments and would be for years to come. Edgar had wanted the rectangle but gave in to Judy, who wanted the classic kidney shape. Kidney, Edgar still felt compelled to point out, was not a shape—it was an organ.

As soon as he was through the front door, Edgar started loosening his tie. None of the other male teachers wore ties, and while Edgar was only a few years past forty, he believed a teacher should wear a tie every day. Even on Fridays.

As he did most days, Edgar crossed the living room and stood in front of the glass-enclosed display case positioned at the far wall. The case held his collection of puzzle boxes—

mostly vintage Japanese personal secret boxes. Gazing at them imparted a touch of the elation he'd felt upon obtaining and solving each one. Edgar looked at them as he finished removing his tie. He was not even aware of this daily ritual. He was not consciously aware that the few seconds he spent standing there drained away much of the day's tension.

He had been collecting them since he was a boy. They ranged from objects of antiquity to sleek modern pieces. His favorites were the Japanese puzzle boxes. Edgar's grandfather had brought one of the trick boxes back from World War II. It was a cheap thing, about half the size of a brick. A touristy trinket decorated with an image of a Japanese boat languishing on a lake with Mount Fuji in the background. The painted decoration was crackled and chipped, and one of the slats was missing from one end. His grandfather had given it to Edgar's father, and Edgar's father had in turn given it to him when Edgar was about twelve. Which sounded more entrenched with meaning than it really was. Nonetheless, Edgar had loved the box. Seemingly a solid block of wood, it was actually a trick box that took six separate moves to open. Putting pressure on just the right part of the box caused a concealed slat to slide. If all the slats were moved in the exact right combination, a hidden compartment would be revealed.

Edgar loved the tactile sensation of them. He loved exerting pressure over the seemingly solid surface only to discover a panel that moved forward. Which led to the discovery of another piece that slid precisely to the side. The next one would need to be moved down. And so on until the puzzle was solved and the secret compartment revealed. His grandfather's box had a hidden compartment as well as a secret drawer that held a 1945 Mercury dime.

Through his teen years, Edgar sought out more such boxes at flea markets and garage sales. As an adult, Edgar had added to the collection and branched out to more modern puzzle boxes as well. He had a solid black cube. A silver orb etched with hieroglyphics—crafted by a magician and touted to be the most difficult puzzle ever created. But mostly, it was the traditional Japanese ones that he craved. With the advent of the Internet, he'd learned that these boxes were still being made, and that the craftsmen who made them were regarded as artists and held places of honor in Japanese society. Edgar owned one that required seventy-eight moves. With eBay, his harmless hobby had blossomed into a bit of an obsession, but a mostly manageable one.

"I hope you're taking that off because you want to put on a better-looking one." Edgar looked at his wife. Judy Woolrich was a tiny thing, and Edgar found the sight of her pleasing even after fifteen years of marriage. She was dressed in a brown skirt and a white silk blouse. The smell of freshly applied perfume stung Edgar's nostrils. It was Joy, purchased in Paris on their tenth wedding anniversary and generally reserved for special occasions.

"Not tonight. I'm tired. Aren't you tired?"

"I most certainly am not tired. And you promised."

"I know, but there's an auction ending tonight and I want to bid on it."

"You're kidding, right? Another auction?"

"This one is special."

"They're all special."

"True, but this one, look, just look."

Edgar pulled up a browser page on the desktop computer at his little home office desk. The desk was just a small thing set up in a cubby in the living room. A place to pay the bills.

"Just look."

In most regards, it was the typical war-era export with Mount Fuji, a lake, and a boat. The sides were a checkerboard marquetry inlay. Quite interestingly, the interior held five separate removable boxes. But what made this truly different, what made it *exceptional*, was that each interior box held an array of tiny treasures, charms, and toys. A tiny dog, a tiny book, a tiny pair of scissors. A complete fifty-two-card deck of miniature playing cards. A Japanese lantern form carved of bone (the lid of which unscrewed to reveal a hidden compartment!). A carved bone geisha figure (that likewise had a hidden compartment that held a miniature pair of bone dice). All handmade. And more. Just so much more. Teakettles, pocketknives. A compass. None of them larger than a pencil eraser. Edgar could hardly believe someone would be willing to sell it.

"There is no way I can let this one slide by."

"So go ahead and bid on it."

"Unh-uh. No way. You know my method."

"Christ, Edgar. What about the iPhone I got you for your birthday? Can't you browse the web on it?"

"True. But I have to keep my eye on the time." Edgar preferred to place his bids in the last few seconds of an auction. He felt that placing an early bid drew attention to a listing and lessened his chances of getting a good deal. "I could do it on the phone browser, but the satellite connection might have a lag. I'd rather do it from home."

"Surely you can adjust for the nanosecond of delay." Judy approached her husband and reknotted his tie for him. "I'll make it worth your while."

"Oh yeah?"

"Yeah." She grabbed hold of the tie, pulled him down to her, and whispered in his ear.

Edgar's eyes got big, and he said, "Isn't that illegal?"

"Not if you're married."

6

GOD FORBID, A BARFLY

Her eyes bright and alert, Helen stared at the bartender, Chuck, who was pointedly ignoring her.

Outside, the green neon sign that read *Smitty's* ticked and burped into life as the last of the daylight drained from the sky.

Smitty's was on Helen's regular rotation. She made it a rule never to patronize any given bar more than once a month, lest she be identified as a regular, or, God forbid, a barfly. She had been avoiding Smitty's for a while now, but she had spotted people she knew in the last three places she had tried.

Helen drummed her fingers on the bar top, cleared her throat, even waved at the man, but it was obvious she was being frozen out.

She thought about Mitzi at home. Since she didn't know if

the dog was a furniture chewer, or how she would be with the cats, Helen had put her in the garage, where it would be dry and warm, with plenty of food and water and a blanket to sleep on. But, really, she should probably have stayed home and helped with the adjustment. The dog was probably scared and nervous. Helen decided that she should just do her drinking at home tonight. She would rather be with her animals. She opened her purse and retrieved her car keys. When she looked up from her purse, the bartender was standing in front of her, staring. She forgot about the animals.

"What?" Helen asked.

The bartender just kept giving her the look.

"What? It couldn't have been that bad. I mean, the place is still standing, right?"

The stare was all she got in return.

"Chuck, c'mon. Was it really that bad? I'm what? Five-five, a hundred and thirty pounds soaking wet? Seriously, how bad could it have been?"

Chuck wasn't going to give in.

"Okay. Okay. I'm sorry. All right? I'm sorry. Honestly. I'm sorry." Helen touched the bartender's arm and gave him her brightest smile.

"Last chance," the man said, and set her up.

7

ABOUT DAMN TIME

He was one of those waiters who made a show out of not writing down orders but relying solely on memory. Edgar found such waitstaff worrisome, but he put it out of his mind and answered the question Judy had asked him moments before.

"Maybe it's because I got picked on a lot at that age," he said. "I don't know. I guess he just, I don't know."

"Reminds you of yourself?"

"Minus the Goth hair, yes, I guess he does."

"I know somebody else who's going to remind you of yourself."

"Future tense?"

Judy nodded.

"Are you kidding? No, of course you're not kidding."

Judy giggled so loud some of the other diners turned to look.

"I'm sure the fertility treatments finally worked. The odds were in our favor. I know it's been years, but statistically the numbers expanded expo—"

"Statistically, Edgar, you knocked me up. And it was about damn time."

8

KARMA AND ITS CHAMELEON-LIKE QUALITIES

Helen squinted through the haze at the man at the end of the bar. Smoking cigarettes was prohibited, but Smitty's used a smoke machine on the tiny dance floor. Helen figured the propylene glycol fog was probably as carcinogenic as tobacco smoke, but right now she really didn't care. It was eighties night at Smitty's, and Culture Club was singing about karma and its chameleon-like qualities.

All was forgiven and bartender Chuck was treating her right: No sooner did she make one Absolut with a lemon zest disappear than he replaced it with a fresh one. She was drinking too fast and knew she'd better slow down. It was early yet, and it had been a long week.

The man sitting at the end of the bar had jet-black hair,

slicked back with some kind of greasy pomade. Mr. Slick-Back sported the hollow-eyed gauntness of a chronic alcoholic, and Helen saw in his eyes what she saw in her own when she woke up in the morning and looked in the mirror. She was drawn to him. They had been playing the game of averted glances for some time now. He was what this Helen wanted. The other Helen, the one who coasted through her day with just enough blood alcohol to keep from getting sick, just enough to keep the schizonucleosis at bay, that Helen would have been repulsed by this greasy caricature. But the secret Helen, the one she kept hidden from the rest of the world, the one who came out only when the booze was flowing freely, this Helen saw her brother and her lover.

The man finally approached her. Maybe he recognized her too.

"May I?"

Helen nodded at the vacant stool.

"My name is Cornell Smith and—"

"Let's not do names."

"I can play that game."

Let's not do names? Helen thought as she slid off her stool. *Oh yeah, I've got a load on.*

"Let's just dance."

Cornell followed Helen onto the dance floor, watching the way her rear bounced ever so nicely. "God damn," he said.

And they danced.

9

HE HOPED THE THREAT OF IT
WOULD BE ENOUGH

If her eyes hadn't been glazed over, her makeup smeared, and her hair tangled, the attractive intelligent woman who had entered the bar a few hours ago might still be recognizable as Helen Patrice, but Helen Patrice was gone, and had been since her fifth drink.

The raunchy opening guitar licks of Def Leppard's "Pour Some Sugar on Me" rumbled through the speakers. The heavy electronic drumbeat kicked in, fueling Helen's alcohol-soaked mind. She and Mr. Slick-Back played tandem air guitar, thrusting and gyrating, crowding the other dancers off the cramped dance space.

The shoulder strap of Helen's camisole top slipped down her shoulder, low enough to expose her breast. She had taken off her bra thirty minutes ago in the ladies' room and shoved it in the garbage bin.

Helen covered herself and readjusted the shoulder strap. Mr. Slick-Back reached out and flicked the strap back off her shoulder, exposing her breast once again. Most of the patrons had stopped whatever they were doing and watched. Helen was unaware, but Mr. Slick-Back was playing it up for the onlookers. He leaned in and playfully bit the top of Helen's exposed breast. She cried out in surprise.

From behind the bar, Chuck watched the spectacle and shook his head. He reached under the counter and grabbed the Louisville Slugger stashed there. He hoped he wouldn't have to use it. He hoped the threat of it would be enough.

10

THE ART OF THE SNIPER BID

A ghost haunting familiar ground, Edgar's white Toyota Camry cruised the scenic coastal highway. The headlights shone in the dark.

In the car, Judy nibbled on Edgar's ear, and he squirmed with feigned annoyance. Judy kept it up, and Edgar glanced at the time on the dashboard.

"Hold on."

Edgar pulled up the web browser on his cell phone. He logged into his eBay account and navigated to the auction page. There were ninety seconds of bidding left. He took the time to scroll through the photos and item details one last time. It was exquisite. Truly a one-of-a-kind puzzle box. And all those hand-made miniatures.

"Eyes on the road, please."

"I'm watching."

"Just let me do it for you. I'm capable."

Of course Judy was capable, but Edgar had the art of the sniper bid down to a science. It had to be timed just right. And a delay had to be factored in when doing it on a cell hookup. Even if it was a nanosecond. He refreshed the page. Still no bids. The starting bid was $350.00, a bit of an expenditure, but a unique box like this one was easily worth thousands. In the listing title, the seller had misspelled Japanese as *Jappanese*, so a lot of people (other collectors with deeper pockets who quite often outbid Edgar and whom he thought of as his "online nemeses") would miss the listing entirely. Edgar maintained listing alerts for keywords like *puzle* and *Japenese*. Sometimes diligence paid off. He felt a stab of excitement; he just might get it at the ridiculously low opening bid.

"You're drifting."

Edgar looked up and corrected the car back to the right of the yellow lines.

He cued up his maximum bid, his finger poised over the "confirm bid" button, gauging for the exact right moment.

The headlights of a passing car momentarily illuminated the interior, making it harder to see the screen.

"Edgar!"

Lights filled the car again. Too bright this time, not passing, but filling the car. Too bright. Edgar looked forward, swerving. Too bright. Too late.

THE MONOTONOUS ELECTRONIC
HUM OF A FLATLINE

The bay doors of the emergency room slammed open as paramedics burst in with a loaded gurney.

Judy Woolrich's body was motionless. Her hair was blackly matted with coagulated blood.

Right behind her, on a second gurney, Edgar was wheeled in. He was very much awake and aware of what was going on, but the paramedics had placed a head stabilization device around his upper body. He could not sit up. He was like a bug on its back. His glasses had been lost in the wreck, and his pale eyes looked alien without them.

Edgar was placed in a treatment room by himself. In the adjoining room, a team of medical personnel worked on his wife. He could hear urgent orders shouted. He could see moving shadows cast through the observation window, but he could not raise himself to see what was happening. He heard the sound of a defibrillation machine cycling up to full charge, and the doctor calmly saying, "Clear." This procedure was repeated several times until there was only the monotonous electronic hum of a flatline.

12

SUBTLE BUT PERMANENT BRAIN DAMAGE

Early sunlight streamed across Helen's closed eyes. The two cats, Molly and Agnes, whom Helen had dubbed "The Yellow and Black Attack" because of their coloring, crisscrossed over her sleeping form, anxious for her to wake up and feed them. For some reason, their owner had failed to keep to the appointed feeding schedule, but even the cats remembered that this had happened before and were not too terribly anxious. This morning, the main source of Molly's and Agnes's anxiety was the Great Dane that had invaded their home and now rested with its head on their owner's pillow.

Mitzi whined and licked Helen's face, saturating it. Helen's breath caught and her bloodshot eyes opened. And the anxiety hit her just that quick. Full-blown panic; her mind raced, the very organs of her body cried out with energy-draining pain. A deep cough racked her chest. It felt like lung tissue had ripped. She remembered the fog machine. Who knew what all chemicals they used in those things? Far worse than secondhand smoke. Small-cell carcinoma. Stage four. Mesothelioma. Emphysema. Black lung. Neurotoxins attacking her synapses. Subtle but permanent brain damage. Cumulative.

No furniture appeared to be chewed on, and there weren't any immediately evident piles of poop, so letting the dog roam free didn't appear to have been too big of an error in judgment. She must have let her into the house when she came in through the garage last night. She let Mitzi out into the fenced backyard, then stumbled into the kitchen, flipped on the television (she needed other voices to compete with the ugly ones in her head), and put coffee on to brew. She opened the refrigerator and grabbed a liter bottle of water. She drank it down and tossed the empty in the trash.

Helen let Mitzi back in, thanking God that Pumpkin Head had at least done a good job housetraining her, then made her way to the bathroom and sat for a long time until she finally urinated. She looked at her output, a dark malodorous yellow, before flushing it away. She was dehydrated. But that was normal. The water would be working its way though her body momentarily. Followed soon after by the cure. Helen stood staring at the commode for no real reason, and once the reservoir tank had refilled itself, the water cut off and she could once again hear the bright cheery voices of the morning news anchors nattering on in the kitchen. Helen glanced at herself in the mirror, not wanting to see her own hollow eyes, but her breast hurt and she needed to look. She lifted her T-shirt and saw a bite mark. She felt shame. Teeth marks on her breast. Disturbing, indeed, but she had awoken to worse. She could almost remember. Something about dancing. Something about that damn fog machine. Mr. Slick-Back. She remembered him. But enough with the reminiscing. Her entire body hurt. It ached. Not wanting to, Helen disrobed completely and examined herself.

The self-inspection did not reveal additional damage. Externally, Helen was still quite attractive—her breasts sagged only a little; her ass, while bigger than in the past, had not succumbed to gravity and was plump in a pleasingly feminine way; and the broken capillaries that formed a haphazard Etch A Sketch across her nose and cheeks were easily concealed with modest amounts of makeup. The shell, the façade, was fine. Unfortunately, she was rotting from the inside out. Like the shiny apple that concealed the corruption of the worm deep inside. It occurred to her hungover mind that she was the perfect hybrid of Doctor Dolittle and Dorian Gray.

Her body emitted certain odors at inopportune times. On occasion, her liver was swollen and tender when palpated, but this faded and flared seemingly without relation to her current intake. She sometimes spit up a thin, watery, bile-like liquid streaked with blood. The blood was particularly worrisome, and she attributed it to either a stomach ulcer or an inflamed esophagus—both conditions attributable to chronic alcohol abuse. She knew that it was not uncommon for profound alcoholics to die of esophageal hemorrhage, and she thought of this whenever she spit up the smeary red liquid. Her legs were often sore and stiff. It was hard to even cross them at times. She suspected it was incipient nerve damage. The beginnings of alcoholic neuropathy.

Quitting, however, was not an option. It was not even a remote thought. A cloud on the horizon. She would live or die on her own terms. Why torture yourself with an unwinnable internal struggle? She didn't necessarily *embrace* who she was, but she certainly accepted it. Sometimes, in the right frame of mind (drunk), she even took pride in it. In fact, Helen had her own personal version of the old U.S. Army recruitment slogan: she drank more before nine A.M. than most people drank all day. Speaking of which, her hands were starting to twitch. Tremor. She needed the cure.

Molly and Agnes, tails like masts, zigged and zagged across the kitchen floor when they heard her popping the metal food cans open. Helen looked at Mitzi. "Will Nine Lives work for you?"

The morning news rattled on. Video footage of a smashed white Toyota Camry being hooked up to a tow truck caught her attention. "—did not survive the accident. Police are asking that anyone with knowledge of the hit-and-run collision to contact them."

A piece of last night flashed through Helen's mind. Just a shard of memory. Of laughter. Laughter cut short as oncoming headlights filled her world.

Like a woman who has heard a prowler in her empty home, Helen made her way down the hall to her garage. Halfway down the hall, her breathing grew labored. She found it hard to catch her breath. Soon she was hyperventilating, drawing the ragged breaths of a sprinter. And with each step, with each hoarse intake of air, a broken image from the previous night emerged from her eclipsed memory. Lights. Faces. Cigarettes. Broken glass. Blood.

She rested her hand on the knob of the door that opened to the garage. After a while, she turned it.

She found the thing that she did not want to find. The front end of her red Honda Insight was accordioned, smashed in. The windshield was cracked over the driver's side.

Helen stooped down to the front grille and picked off a fleck of white paint embedded there. She stared at the chip of paint balanced on her fingernail. In her mind, a word glowed, and that word was: *evidence.*

Greasy sweat popped out on her forehead. She clamped her hand to her mouth, but it wasn't enough to stem the flow of guilt and vomit as it erupted through her fingers.

She ran back through the house to the bathroom. Vomiting the whole way.

THE SWEET ODOR
OF THE CONDUCTING GEL

Edgar looked at his wife's body laid out on the hospital bed. The blood had been cleaned from her face and hair. Her hair had been combed. It looked wrong. Judy had been very particular about her hair.

An IV catheter remained in her arm; the plastic tubing taped down, connected to nothing.

Edgar sat in a rigid plastic-and-metal chair. He wore a cumbersome neck brace. The doctor had said that Edgar's intervertebral joints were likely inflamed, but the scan revealed no true injury. The brace was a prophylactic measure and should also ease some of the discomfort.

Sitting directly next to Edgar in an identical chair was Jane Ketchum, Judy's sister. Jane was holding Edgar's hand. Jane had been the only call Edgar had made. She and Judy had been particularly close. They talked every night, even if only for a few minutes. And most weekends, Edgar and Judy would have Jane and her husband, Steve, over to play Rook or spades.

Jane and Edgar had been sitting in the hospital room with Judy's body for more than two hours. They were waiting for the representative of the funeral home to arrive and take possession of the body. The body. There it was. That was what Judy had now become. The body. The remains. What was left after life had departed.

He and Jane had already said the things that needed saying. There had been hugging and crying and smeary mascara stains left on Edgar's shirt. But for now, there was nothing left to say. For now they sat side by side and held hands in silence and waited and thought their private thoughts.

Edgar was cataloging all of the bad things he had done in the course of his life. All the wrongs. There were some. Plenty, even. But they didn't add up. The equation didn't balance. He was a good man. An honest and accountable man. But that had not always been so. There had been life lessons. Mistakes were made. Every shitty little thing he'd ever done played through Edgar's mind: the tests cheated on, the cat he'd kicked as a child, the boy he'd picked on in junior high, the car he'd backed into and left without leaving a note, and just a few years ago, the teacher he'd almost had an affair with—there were plenty of bad things, sure, but there was no way in hell they added up to Judy dead, his unborn child dead with her. How could they? Would God do that? Would God kill them to get at Edgar? There was no sense to it. No way to find equilibrium. Unless. Unless the cheated tests counted. Unless the almost-affair counted. Unless it all added up. Accumulated. Each little transgression amplified by the one before. All of it adding up and counting blackly against him. But maybe if there was just one thing, maybe it was Mark Pitts. The boy. Eighth grade. Why had he joined in the torment of Mark? That was not who he was. That was not Edgar Woolrich. Yet it had been. He had been that person. He'd joined in. He'd swung his fists. He had spit on Mark. His hand had been there, holding him down as others pushed Mark's head into the feces-fouled toilet. It was not who he was, but, yes, he'd joined in. He'd ruined the boy, glad it was not himself being humiliated, ruined. Glad to be part of the group, not the lone target.

So maybe it did all add up. An accumulation of sins, paid for in one fell swoop. Maybe this was retribution. Perhaps it genuinely was equilibrium. If there was a finger of blame to be pointed, it was Edgar who stood accused. Yes, in the end, it was his fault. He had cost them their lives (the one life never realized). Oh, Jesus Christ, he was to blame. He'd done it.

But no, he rejected that. It was self-pity. It had been a hit-and-run driver. The police had said so. They'd questioned him. He did not tell them that he had been looking at the display on his cell phone. What he told them was that the other car had crossed the line, drifted into Edgar's lane. He did not know whether this was true but felt certain it was. What *was* true, and what Edgar further told the police, was that the other vehicle had fled the scene of the accident without offering help.

Two men entered the room. The men were wearing dark suits and plastic badges that identified them as attendants from the funeral home Jane had called.

"Mr. Woolrich?"

Edgar uncoupled his hand from Jane's and rose stiffly from his chair. He shook hands with the man who had spoken. The man handed Edgar a pen and a clipboard. The other attendant motioned a third man into the room. This third attendant wheeled in a gurney with the funeral home's logo and a purple velvet pad on top.

Edgar handed the pen and clipboard back to the first man, having signed the release for his wife's body.

"You're welcome to ride with us, Mr. Woolrich."

"No."

"Would you like a minute before we transport Mrs. Woolrich?"

"Yes."

The men left the room. Jane Ketchum followed them out.

Edgar took Judy's hand and squeezed it just a bit, aware of the absence of life. He could smell hospital odors. He could smell antiseptic and adhesive, and underneath that the sweet odor of the conducting gel used for the defibrillator paddles. And underneath that, Edgar could smell her perfume, Joy.

14

COVERING UP HER CRIME

Dressed in cutoff jeans and a T-shirt, Helen bent over the front of her car with a stiff wire brush. She scrubbed the painted surface until only bare metal was showing. Sweat dripped from her nose, and strings of her hair clung to her wet face.

She stood back and looked. She was satisfied that there was no evidence of the white paint from the other car.

In the backseat she found twelve cans of Natural Light—seven empties and five unopened. She seldom drank beer and didn't remember stopping to get it. Under one of the cans she found two teeth—central incisors, they looked like—stuck to the floor mat in a congealed pool of blood and spit. She put them in the trash with everything else.

* * *

She drove across the state line. She stopped at a phone booth that had a Yellow Pages directory hanging from a chain. She dismissed the larger places, the national chains, and found a small place that felt right to her.

Helen sat in the grimy waiting room. The television mounted to the wall had antenna reception through a digital converter box, and the picture rolled. The magazines were years out of date and yellowed with nicotine and age. She was in the right place. No computers. No online database.

The man behind the front desk was chain-smoking unfiltered Camels. Helen glanced at him and saw that he was staring at her legs in her cutoffs. She tucked her legs together and placed a magazine in her lap. The man kept staring. Finally, Helen said, "Get an eyeful?"

The counterman raised an eyebrow and shrugged.

"You think my legs look good?"

The man nodded and smiled.

"Wonder how they would look sticking out of your ass."

The man made a great show of putting away his paperwork before stomping away and calling Helen "trash."

Helen got up and walked to the tiny window overlooking the repair area and watched two repairmen buffing down the hood where the crinkled metal had been hammered out. Another repairman was applying the last of the sealant to the newly installed windshield.

Once the repairs were complete, Helen drove to a high-end body and paint shop. She paid the shop manager three hundred dollars to put her at the head of the line. The color of her Honda Insight was changed from red to black, including doorjambs, under the hood, and a factory-look clearcoat. It cost thirty-five hundred dollars, which Helen paid from a cash advance on her American Express.

The various coats and something called "baking time" normally took three days, but, for the extra cash, the manager promised an overnight turnaround. He would have to bring in a technician to finish it up on Sunday, which cost Helen an additional three hundred on top of what she had already paid. She considered it a bargain. And she had a feeling that since she was paying everything in cash, this whole transaction would never find its way onto the shop's records.

She spent the night in a hotel. Mostly sober. Worried about her pets. But she had nobody she could call to check in on them. To let the dog out. To put down food. She had not arranged her life for such things.

Through all of this, Helen had not allowed herself to reflect on what she had done or what she was now doing. She allowed herself to consider only the immediate task. That of covering up her crime.

15

SOYLENT GREEN IS PEOPLE

Helen took one last look at her shiny, newly painted, black car before turning off the garage light and stepping back into the house. The accident had happened on Friday. She'd had the car repaired and repainted on Saturday and Sunday, and tomorrow she would have to explain why she'd decided to have her car repainted a new color. She could have had the Honda painted the same red color so as not to draw attention to herself, but that seemed too risky to her. If white paint had transferred to her car, then her red paint had certainly transferred to the car she had hit. The police would be looking for a red car. As she had been in a blackout at the time, she had no way of knowing if there had been witnesses. If someone had witnessed the accident, then the police could very well be looking for a red Honda

Insight. If someone had gotten the license plate, then it would have been the police waking her up Saturday morning instead of Mitzi. If the police had a partial plate, then they wouldn't go to the trouble of running hers if she was driving the wrong color car. No, it would be far safer to draw the curiosity of her staff (she didn't have any friends) than to risk being on the road with too many identifiers.

Helen plopped onto the couch and broke the seal on a fifth of vodka. She had gone an entire day without drinking. Just the maintenance nips, but those didn't count. Those were just so she could keep her shit together and do what needed to be done. But she hadn't got properly drunk. And her body was in turmoil. She was not allowing herself to apply rational thought to this. It was simply what she must do. She poured two inches into her glass and settled back to enjoy it.

Molly and Agnes crawled over the back of the couch. Helen reached up and rubbed their bellies.

She filled her glass again. Three inches this time.

After a while, Helen crawled to the floor and wrestled with Mitzi. The Great Dane could pin her easily.

She crawled back over to the vodka and refilled her glass. She picked up the newspaper and read the same column of newsprint for perhaps the twentieth time. It was Judy Woolrich's obituary.

Later, Helen watched an old movie on television: *Soylent Green*. She watched as bulldozers scooped up America's overpopulation while Charlton Heston tried to control the mobs. And Edward G. Robinson checked himself into a suicide center. He was laid out on a gurney watching nature scenes projected on an oversized screen, waiting for his lethal cocktail to kick in.

From time to time, Helen would pick up the folded newspaper and look yet again at the obituary and accompanying photo of Judy Woolrich. Helen looked at the photo and then at Edward G. Robinson. She screamed.

Helen grabbed the lamp from a side table and smashed the porcelain base to pieces. She freed the electrical cord from the wall and gathered it up. She scanned the room, looking. Her eyes were beyond bloodshot. They were vacant. Helen was gone.

Finally, her gaze settled on the ceiling fan/light fixture. She fashioned the cord into a crude loop and placed it around her neck. She used a kitchen chair to stand on and tied the other end of the cord to the ceiling fan. Helen looked down at Mitzi and said, "Bye." She kicked the chair away. And by some obscene miracle, the half-assed noose worked. Helen hung suspended, her breathing cut off. In that moment, a rational thought penetrated her alcohol-benumbed mind: She had forgotten about the animals. Who would feed them? Who would take care of them? This was a mistake, she realized. But by then the booze and lack of oxygen had shut down this avenue of coherent thought.

After about forty-five seconds, Helen's legs kicked in a muscle spasm. The ceiling fan creaked. Then gave way.

Helen fell to the floor. The ceiling fan landed inches from her head but left her unmarked. Her breath was ragged, coarse, but there. Mitzi, scared away by the crashing fixture, cautiously returned and licked her unconscious new owner. Molly and Agnes, more cautious, watched from a reasonable distance.

On the television, Charlton Heston screamed, "Soylent Green is people! It's people!"

16

IT DIDN'T LOOK VERY GOOD AT ALL

Outside Edgar's well-kept Dutch Colonial home, people came and went. Cars filled the driveway and spilled out onto the street.

Inside, hams and casserole dishes overflowed the dining room table. The funeral had ended an hour ago, and most of the people were wearing suits and dresses. Edgar sat in his well-worn leather recliner and let the mourners come to him. He accepted them as a head of state might. They patted and hugged and stroked him and kissed him lightly on the cheek. He accepted those gestures with grace. His motions were stiff, partly due to the neck brace.

Principal Cleage, around bites of chicken wing, talked to a

group of teachers from the school. They all laughed at something Cleage said.

Jane Ketchum emerged from the kitchen and grabbed Edgar
by the hand, extracting him from his chair. In the kitchen was
Jane's husband, Steve, as well as their children: Tyler, seven, and
Savannah, four. Judy had wanted children from day one, but,
Edgar remembered, she had never once shown resentment over
Jane's children. Judy had attended each of their births and
spoiled the children as a grandmother might.

Jane presented Edgar with a large packing carton. She
opened it and showed him that it was packed full with Tupperware containers of individual meals she had prepared for him.

Tyler grabbed one of the containers and pried off its lid to
peek inside. Jane snatched it from him. "Goddamn it, Tyler,
stop it!" Edgar had heard her say worse to the children. "Take
Savannah outside to play. And stay away from the pool."

Tyler complied, taking his sister's hand and heading out
the back door. "I'll go watch them," Steve said, and followed
them out.

Jane began transferring the containers from the carton to
the freezer.

"Listen, Edgar, each one of these has a complete meal in it,
okay? All you have to do is put it in the microwave. Ten minutes
if it's frozen, five if it's thawed."

She showed him the contents of one of the containers. It
contained pale turkey, tired-looking green peas, and a blob of
mashed potatoes. To Edgar, it didn't look very good at all.

"Now I'm going to bring you some more in a couple of weeks. And we're going to help you any way we can."

"Jane, this isn't necessary. Judy was your sister. You're not—"

"Goddamn it, Edgar! Just let me help you."

"You're not responsible for her husband. And you have your own husband. And kids."

Jane stuck her fingers in her ears and said, "Na-na-na-na-na-na-na-na. I'm not listening to you. You're getting this food, so shut up about it, okay?"

Jane hugged him, but Edgar didn't really respond.

17

AN ACCUMULATION
OF RADIOACTIVE ISOTOPES

One of the cars lining Edgar's street, just beyond the mass of mourner vehicles, was a black Honda Insight.

Helen watched people come and go. Her fingers played lightly along the red welt around her neck.

Helen started the car and drove away. She left the old section of town and entered the main strip with its shopping plazas. She drove to Jerry's Liquor Warehouse.

Inside, Helen pushed a metal shopping cart up and down the wide aisles. Fluorescent lights flickered and buzzed high overhead. The harsh light was unkind to the scabbed ring around her neck. She had closed the veterinary clinic for a few days. When she reopened, she was hoping the injury would have healed enough that she could conceal it with makeup. The scab ring was too high up on her neck to conceal with clothing unless she alternated between turtleneck sweaters and Elizabethan collars.

She did not remember doing it, but the evidence when she woke up had been self-explanatory.

Seemingly every kind of booze known to man was on display. Whiskey, gin, rum, tequila, bourbon, brandy, scotch, schnapps, and, of course, vodka. Helen had decided it was time to take a break from vodka. It was affecting her judgment. Plus the blackouts. Oh, and killing somebody. Mustn't forget that. Or that trying-to-kill-yourself thing. Right, the suicide attempt. Vodka was definitely not agreeing with her.

Helen selected a bottle of light rum and a bottle of scotch. Her mother had drunk scotch. She approached the checkout aisle and then changed her mind. She returned the rum and the scotch. She picked up a liter bottle of vodka. But not Absolut. It must be something about the Absolut that was warping her mind. Vodka had never bothered her before. Absolut was made in Russia. It was made from grain. She was pretty sure the Chernobyl disaster had occurred in Russia, or Ukraine—which amounted to the same thing. All that radioactive waste was released when the nuclear reactor melted down. But no, Absolut was made in Sweden. Said it right on the bottle. But weren't all those countries kind of clustered right there together? She was pretty sure they were. Helen remembered reading that four hundred times more fallout was released from Chernobyl than had been created by the atomic bombing of Hiroshima. A giant cloud of it had drifted all over the top half of Europe. And radioactivity lasted for hundreds of years. Thousands. If the grain that was used to produce Absolut was grown in Sweden or Ukraine or Russia, who was to say that it couldn't possibly be contaminated grain? Who was to say that her mind hadn't been poisoned with an accumulation of radioactive isotopes? It had all started with the schizonucleosis. Then the blackouts. It made sense. Sure, it was probably low doses, but when it came to radiation, accumulation was the key. *Accumulation*. Did the Swedes even drink Absolut? Or was it all exported to the United States? No, they wouldn't push that poison on their own people. Sell it to the stupid Americans. They'll drink anything.

Something was certainly going on with her. She knew it sounded crazy, but alcohol, and in particular vodka, had never been a true problem for her. She was functional. She had always been functional.

Helen chose Grey Goose vodka. It was made in France. The French knew what the fuck they were doing. And they were upwind from the radiation cloud. The more she thought about it, the angrier she grew.

She took her Grey Goose and placed it in front of the bearded clerk at the checkout counter. The man, who had apparently been observing her, said, "Tough choice?"

Helen felt herself getting ready to unload on the man. Say something smart and ugly. But the anger she had felt was followed by relief. She realized that maybe the things that had been happening to her were very likely not truly her fault. She was a victim as well. *Accumulation*.

She shook her head and handed the man her debit card.

18

WEIRD SCI-FI SHIT

The television was tuned to Animal Planet. Helen had decided that she didn't need any more weird sci-fi shit fucking with her mind. It put ideas in your head.

She watched the television, the unopened vodka bottle resting next to a drinking glass on the coffee table in front of her. Mitzi, her body on the floor and her head in Helen's lap, looked up at her owner. One of the cats, Molly, a black-and-white long-hair with hypnotic green eyes (she was the black half of The Yellow and Black Attack), jumped on the coffee table and wove expertly between the glass and bottle of Grey Goose. Helen chose to believe that it was the cat that had drawn her attention to the vodka. She chose to believe that she had forgotten that it was there, but now that she had been reminded about it, there was certainly nothing wrong with having a drink in the privacy of your own home.

She deserved it. It was hard work covering up vehicular homicide.

And stressful.

In fact, it was Absolut Murder—LOL ha-ha-ha-ha-ha ROFLMFAO.

She needed a drink. Deserved a drink. She was going to have a drink.

Then she could think about it. Then she could allow her mind to reflect. But she forced herself to think about it anyway.

When she thought of the taking of a human life, what it meant, Helen found the whole concept bigger than her mind was capable of processing. She simply could not internalize that particular truth.

You could perpetrate all manner of violence—the most unspeakable of horrors—against another human being, but in the end, they were still left as human beings. The spark of life remained. A rape victim could be stripped of her dignity, her sense of safety, and left a shattered shut-in, her life irrevocably altered—but still, she did have life. That had not been taken.

Parents of brain-damaged children (casualties of sporting accidents, car wrecks, drug overdoses) still had their children even if the once-vibrant sons and daughters they had formerly cherished were gone forever, wiped out with a bit of cerebral tissue, wisped away with the oxygen that had been denied. They still had a living thing to touch and hold and kiss.

But once life was gone, all was lost. There was no hope.

Had it not been her own sense of life, her own self-preservation that had driven her to conceal what she had done? To cleanse herself of culpability. To say to the world, *No, not me, I had nothing to do with this.*

And now, she only wanted to cleanse her mind of this unspeakable burden. Alcohol, the most versatile of the chemical solvents, was, Helen knew, the preeminent Windex of the mind. Albeit a temporary one. Yes, alcohol gave a streak-free shine to even the most occluded of brains. It dislodged the dirt. And if the grime of misdeeds was back in the morning, sullying one's placidity yet again, why, there was always the next night, wasn't there? Ask any housewife: Things don't stay clean forever; you have to keep cleaning them over and over.

But killing another human being was different, wasn't it? There was no escaping it. The booze couldn't clean that knowledge away. Drinking only magnified. It opened the chasm. It gave you the courage to look. It made your mind capable of processing the truth. And that was too much to accept.

Needed a drink. Deserved a drink. Going to have a drink.

There was no escape.

Helen snatched the bottle off the table and carried it to the kitchen. All of the animals followed her. Helen stood over the kitchen sink. She studied the bottle. Then she peered into the drain of the sink.

She took the bottle back to the living room and sat down with it. She pressed it to her forehead, feeling the smooth cool glass. It was like bone. She rubbed the bottle over her face, smearing her makeup.

Helen carried the bottle to her bedroom and climbed into bed still holding it. She cradled it like an infant.

Many hours later, Helen slept.

19

SWOLLEN BLACK BODIES

An oily, foul-smelling sweat glistened sickly on her forehead. It covered her body. It stung the corners of her eyes. Helen could feel her pulse in her wrists, hot and insistent. She just couldn't figure out what to do with herself. If she wasn't going to have a drink, what was there to do? What exactly would she do? There was no answer. It was like looking into an abyss. And yes, the abyss looked back. The abyss wondered just what the fuck was she going to do with herself if she wasn't going to drink. What was there to do? How could she exist?

That was the beginning. The existential puzzle of the dry drunk. And there was no answer. Except the obvious. You do nothing. If you don't drink, you do nothing. She'd done a sober night here, an alcohol-free day there. Mostly to repair. To recuperate. But this was different. This was staring into the infinite despair of a life without drinking. Life without the cure for it. Where was the hope? Where was the pleasure? What was the point? There was no point.

When the hallucinations started, Helen denied them. There was simply no way she could be having hallucinations. It was not possible. She was not *that kind* of alcoholic. This had to be something more akin to a visual disturbance. A waking dream. She was *functional*, goddamn it! She was not some fucking grizzled stew bum.

But the spiders disagreed. They were emerging from the shadows, high in the corners where the walls and ceiling met. Just crawling out of the darkness with thick, juice-plumped black legs, dragging their bloated, venom-laden bodies down the wall, making their way to Helen's feet—which she was, for some reason, unable to move. She watched in frozen horror as they inched up her legs, and up her arms, their dripping stingers at the ready. *But no*, some part of her mind reminded her, *this is not real. Spiders don't have stingers. Except these do*, another part of her mind answered. *These are special. These were incubated in the hot radioactive dregs of discarded vodka bottles. Mutations hatched for you. Borne of you.*

Still unable to move, Helen watched the black hairy stingers penetrating her flesh. But there was no pain. No pain because they were not stingers after all. They were some kind of un-natural proboscides. Their function was to suck blood. To feed from her. And now she could feel it, except the sensation was not of something leaving her body, of something being drained from her—but of something going in, something being left behind. They were laying eggs. *Eggs.* Beneath her skin, laying eggs. She was the host.

Helen's long-deceased Uncle Billy knelt in front of her, his kind face alight with a comforting smile. *You can move now*, he told her. *Just brush them off. That's right, sweetgirl, just brush them right off. They can't hurt you. You're okay.*

And he was right. She could move her body. And the spiders flicked right off. No problem. *Oh, thank you, Uncle Billy.*

You're welcome, sweetgirl. Those spiders can't hurt you.

No, they can't.

From his kneeling position in front of her, Uncle Billy held out his hand. Helen looked down at it. His hand was thick, the fingers plump and callused. Helen took his hand. And they were in the water together. She was just a little girl. This was a mem-ory. She could see the dense mat of curly gray hair that covered Uncle Billy's chest. It was coarse and wet with chlorinated pool water. Under the hair he had saggy man-boobs. He was just an old man. Helen floated on her back in the water; Billy's thick arms (also matted in dense gray hair) supported her, kept her from sinking. And she was scared. She was scared of sinking. She couldn't swim. Billy was teaching her. Teaching her how to swim. She trusted him. It felt good to be in his arms. Safe. He took one hand away and told her to kick her legs. *See, you're practically swimming now. Just keep kicking. One at a time. Hold your arms out. See.*

She was moving through the water. Gliding. Swimming. Just Billy's one arm supporting her. She was swimming! Then the hand Billy had taken away was on her thigh. Moving up. It found its way to the V between her legs. Grabbing her roughly. Ugly gouging fingers. Rough and hurtful. Why? *Be quiet*, he told her. *Just be quiet*. And he pulled her open. His fat fingers opening her. Then the spiders came out. The spiders came out and their swollen black bodies covered them both.

20

I NEED FOR YOU TO NOT TALK TO ME

Elmore held a Yorkshire terrier on the exam table while Helen attempted to get the proper placement of a Schirmer test strip in the dog's lower eye. The dog had developed a thick, yellowish discharge from her eyes—pretty common in Yorkies. She likely had KCS, deficient tear production. The lack of tears allowed bacterial organisms to overgrow the eye. The Schirmer test strip would allow Helen to confirm that KCS was behind the chronic eye infections. It was simply a small strip of absorbent material that was placed inside the dog's lower eyelid. The strip would change color as it absorbed tears, and Helen could then measure it against normal values.

Typically, it was an easy test, and Helen could not remember ever having this level of difficulty in placing the strip in a dog's eye. Elmore was doing his part and held the Yorkie's head perfectly still, but every time Helen attempted to get the strip placed inside the lower eyelid, her hand shook too much to perform the task. At one point she had scratched the dog's cornea. The dog whimpered, and so did the nervous owner. Yorkshire terriers tended to be high strung, and so did the people who owned them. Helen decided to try one last time, but as soon as she got close to the dog's eye, her hand trembled like she had Parkinson's disease. She was very much aware that Elmore was likewise very much aware that something was, alas, very much wrong.

"You know what? I seem to be having a bad morning. There's no reason to put Francesca through this. I'm certain that it's KCS like we talked about. I'm going to prescribe cyclosporine drops. Three times a day. If you don't see an improvement within two weeks, I want you to bring Francesca back."

Helen stood outside the clinic building near the rear fire exit. She had stopped on her way to work that morning and bought a pack of cigarettes. Normally, she never smoked at work. It wasn't professional. She took one out and lit it. She had to have something to settle her nerves.

The midmorning sun was shining directly on the building, and the bricks had already absorbed a good bit of heat. It felt good to her. And the smoke felt good in her lungs.

The steel exit door creaked open, and Helen ditched her cigarette, but not before Elmore saw her.

"Caught you."

Helen shrugged.

"Little shaky in there."

"We all have bad days, Elmore."

"Some are worse than others."

Helen nodded.

"If you ever want to talk, I'm here."

"Are you sure you want to do this with me? Are you sure you want to play amateur psychologist?"

"Right. Sorry."

Helen lit a fresh cigarette. Elmore motioned for one as well. She gave it to him and offered him a light.

She couldn't figure out how to interact with human beings without alcohol flowing through her veins. How did people talk to one another without a buzz? How was that possible? Where did they find the courage? The motivation? Anytime you interacted with another person, you were putting yourself at risk. You were opening yourself to criticism, derision, or even downright hatred. She wondered how this could be tolerated without booze soothing your brain, telling you it didn't matter what other people thought of you.

How could life be lived without alcohol? What was the point?

Elmore said, "You know, we never have as many secrets as we think we do. People figure things out. When I told my parents that I'm gay, they were like, we were wondering when you were going to tell us. I had built up in my mind that it would be this huge shock to them, but they had always known. They were just waiting for me to catch up."

"That's a touching story. They should print it up in *The Advocate*. Really. But not now, okay? Now is not the time for a Hallmark moment. I need for you to not talk to me."

Elmore gathered his courage. Dr. Patrice was not one to share aspects of her personal life. Their relationship had always been an easy one, but this was new ground he was breaking.

"I've smelled the booze on your breath." That one just kind of hung out there for a minute, kind of like the *Hindenburg* hung out there before it exploded. Elmore lit the match: "People think that vodka's odorless. But it's not. And I'll tell you what smells even worse. Not drinking. A drunk who stops drinking smells sour. That's how you smell. That's how I used to smell. Sour."

Helen stared at Elmore, waiting for the anger to subside enough for her to speak. To speak in a tone that would not belie her emotions. She did not want him to know that his words had found their target.

"You should share all these observations, bons mots, and life experiences with your career counselor at the unemployment office. I'll mail your last check. Good-bye."

21

THE DRONING ROBOT

Still wearing his neck brace, Edgar drew a triangle on the chalkboard. He labeled the sides *A*, *B*, and *C*. He turned to face the class. He looked at his students for a moment and realized he didn't know what to say, so he picked up his textbook and began to read, covering the same material yet again. He just couldn't get past triangles or his old friend, Pythagoras.

"The Pythagorean theorem posits an absolute truth in regard to not only the world, but the . . ." Despite the fact that he was reading, Edgar lost his train of thought. "Universe. The Pythagorean theorem asserts that . . ."

In the back of the class, the trouble spot, Jack Mendelson, pulled a wet wad of purple bubble gum out of his mouth and dropped it down the back of Martin's shirt. Two onlookers snickered, then laughed out loud when Mendelson shoved his fist into Martin's back—setting the gum. Edgar looked up and saw it happen, but he was having such difficulty maintaining his thoughts that he decided to keep moving forward with the lesson and deal with behaviors later.

"That is, the theorem asserts that for a right triangle, the square of the hypotenuse is equal to the sum of the squares of the other two sides."

Notes were passed. Girls whispered. Boys drew. No one listened to the droning robot teaching this class.

22

MEALS FOR ONE

Edgar pushed a shopping cart through the frozen foods section. He just couldn't stomach Jane's cooking. The grocery store's prepackaged meals were only marginally better.

Edgar's cart was almost half full. In sharp contrast to the piles of items in the other shoppers' carts, Edgar had arranged his goods in a very ordered, almost geometric design. Nothing was out of place.

As he pushed the cart, one of his items shifted out of place. Edgar stopped and rearranged all of the items until everything was packed in a tight precise construction that could easily withstand a trip through a war zone.

At the checkout, while Edgar waited his turn, he loaded his selections on the conveyor belt that would transport the food to the cash register. He noted a pattern. Certain words and phrases that appeared over and over again. *Meals for one. Solos. Single serving.*

THESE PEOPLE WERE INSANE

It was a church basement set up with tight rows of folding chairs and a folding table off to the side set up with a coffee urn and foam cups. There were about forty chairs, and roughly half of them held occupants—mostly white with a scattering of other races, and about equally split with men and women of different ages.

A fiftyish woman with frizzy salt-and-pepper hair and wearing a maroon velour tracksuit stood up. "My name is Martha and I'm an alcoholic."

"Hi, Martha," the group responded in unison.

A teenage girl with a bright red patch of acne engulfing her chin stood up. "My name is Pearl and I'm an alcoholic." The group welcomed her, and Pearl added, "I also enjoy crack and hydrocodone."

A man with muttonchop sideburns went next. He said his name was Walter and that this was his first meeting. Even though he elected to forgo the usual declaration, he was welcomed heartily. Then there was an older woman whose finger was set in a splint and wrapped with white gauze.

Helen wondered if the woman with the finger splint had fallen and broken her finger while she was drunk. And the girl with acne was downright odd. It was like she was placing the worst sort of personal ad: *I like sunny days, long walks on the beach, and I also enjoy crack and hydrocodone. Let's get together.* And speaking of odd, hadn't muttonchops gone the way of Jack the Ripper? Helen was more certain than ever that she didn't belong here. Maybe she could slip out before it was her turn to stand up. Or just do like Jack the Tippler and say that it was her first meeting, thank you, and keep on moving. Yes, she could do that, but then everyone would think of her just exactly what she had thought of old Jack: that he didn't yet have the balls to say it, to say that he was an alcoholic.

Maybe she could try explaining to them that she had been one of the invisible victims of radiation poisoning.

Taped on the wall above the coffee urn was an edge-worn poster. It listed the twelve steps of Alcoholics Anonymous. Step one stated: *We admitted we were powerless over alcohol—that our lives had become unmanageable.* Okay, right there, Helen already had a problem. Yes, fine, she was an alcoholic. She had come to terms with that years ago. And if it made these people feel gushy inside, then she could stand up and state just that. No problem. The issue was that her life was certainly not unmanageable. She was a college graduate. She had obtained her doctor of veterinary medicine degree. She owned her own home, her own vet practice. Hardly the hallmarks of a skid row derelict straining Sterno through a befouled pair of underwear. Yes, she was an alcoholic, but she was a *functional* alcoholic.

Step two: *Came to believe that a Power greater than ourselves could restore us to sanity.* Sure. Why not?

Step three: *Made a decision to turn our will and our lives over to the care of God as we understood Him.* Okay. Fine. God is great. God is good.

Step four: *Made a searching and fearless moral inventory of ourselves.* She could see where that might present a challenge.

Step five: *Admitted to God, to ourselves, and to another human being the exact nature of our wrongs.* Hold the phone. Do what? Fuck that shit. She'd just finished covering up a crime; confessing that to somebody didn't seem the most prudent course of action. These people were insane.

Helen quickly scanned the remaining steps and thought, *Jesus Christ, that's a lot of shit to do.* No wonder AA worked for so many people—who would have time to drink? It was just too much. Coming here had been a horrible mistake. A stupid mistake. She wasn't in her right mind. She was sweating. Her heart was racing. Her hands were trembling. It had to be the radiation.

It was her turn. Helen stood up. "My name is Helen. And I drink. A lot. I enjoy it. I enjoy it so much, I thought I might have a problem. But coming here tonight, I think maybe that it's all

of you who have a problem. Honestly, and don't take this the
wrong way, but, uh, when you took that moral inventory, did you
write down that you're all just a bunch of pathetic assholes? I
mean, for Christ's sake, put yourselves out of your misery. Have
a drink. That's what I'm going to do." With that, Helen turned
and fought past the knees of the people sitting in her row.

The woman wearing the maroon jogging suit stood up and
followed Helen out of the meeting. In the anteroom, Helen was
opening the door to leave. The woman, Martha, caught up
with her.

"Wait!"

Helen turned and arched an eyebrow in questioning
annoyance.

"My name is Martha."

"And you're an alcoholic. I know. I get it."

"No, you don't get it. In fact, you got it completely wrong,
my dear. We did put ourselves out of our misery. We stopped
drinking."

"Is that velour?"

"You're goddamn right it's velour. I dress for comfort, not
style."

Helen smiled.

"And you're quite right about another thing. Quite right. We
are a bunch of pathetic assholes. Welcome to the club."

"Yes, I'm an asshole too, but I'm not quite ready to join up.
To make it official. Thanks just the same."

"Suit yourself, but really, isn't it a little silly to not at least
sit through one meeting? Are you scared you'll catch sobriety

through osmosis? I wish it were that easy. I'll sit with you. Come on."

"I can't go back in there. I made a fool of myself in front of those people."

"Dear, my first meeting, I stood up, said, 'Hi, my name is Martha,' and then I threw up all over myself. If I can come back after that, you can too."

24

CHAOS AND CRIME

Detective Lydia Poole looked up at her partner, Detective Alvin Miller, and groaned. Miller had cocked his thumb over toward the detective bureau's waiting area. When Poole looked in that direction, she saw Edgar Woolrich sitting on the long wooden bench, a stuffed manila envelope resting on his lap. She had gotten so used to seeing him with the neck brace that he looked somehow naked to her now that he no longer wore it. Woolrich looked up, and before Poole could look away, he had caught her eye. *Damn.* She faked a smile and waved him over.

"Mr. Woolrich, good afternoon. I'm sorry, but we don't have any update for you. Your case is still active, but it's cold. I'm sorry that's all I have for you."

Edgar thrust the bulging manila envelope into her hands.

"More charts?" Poole opened the envelope and pulled out a sheaf of papers containing graphs, charts, and equations.

"I've been looking into chaos theory. Are you familiar with it? Or maybe the theory of chaos and crime? In any given form of crime, chaos theory tells us that we look for small changes in ordinary variables. Perhaps external variables. Simple things such as car color likelihoods, or what individuals are attracted to what colors. We look for nonlinear transformations in the behavior of complex systems. You can't find someone based on what colors they like. I mean that's just nonsense, right? Unless you believe in chaos. Non. Linear. Transformations. That's critical. Nonlinear. Do you realize—"

"Okay, wait a minute. Wait a minute. We've been down this road. Police work will solve this, okay? If it's solvable, police work will solve it. That's the way I see it. I'm sorry."

"If you translate traffic patterns and automaker statistics into a three-dimensional binary grid—I mean, just the fact that the other car was red fills in over half the grid right off the bat."

"Fine. You're a math teacher, right? There are forty thousand paint samples on record at the National Automotive Paint File. This shade of red involved in your accident—"

"There are no accidents."

"—is used by three major makers on eleven models. We've looked into this. You know this already. The clear topcoat has been in use since ninety-nine. Do you have any idea how many cars that works out to? Millions. Tens of millions, maybe. Without a witness, we only have the physical evidence. We only have the pool of matching red cars to direct us. You have any idea how many red cars are on the road at any given time?"

"No, I don't know."

"I'm sorry, but we are still trying. We are still looking. But don't get your hopes up. It's cold now. At least that's the way I see it. All I can do is be honest with you."

Poole handed the papers back to Edgar and bid him a good day.

25

RECTANGLES OF WHITE LIGHT

The scenic coastal highway used to calm him, but these days Edgar mostly avoided it whenever he could. His car now sat parked on the shoulder of the highway, engine running, hazard lights blinking. It was dark now. He had been here several hours.

He sat and counted cars.

The paper on his lap was crowded with slash marks. One column, the one designated *All Others*, had hundreds, perhaps a thousand slashes. The column headed *Red* had perhaps an eighth of that number.

Edgar closed his eyes for a moment, and a car passing by pushed rectangles of white light across his face. He could see the light, magnified through his eyeglasses and filtered red through his closed eyelids. Edgar remembered Judy. In the car with Judy. *Eyes on the road, please*, she had said. He noticed now how the light from the oncoming car was fleshly red, warm and welcoming like Judy, then white and accusatory.

His eyes snapped open as another car passed. He marked it down on his chart.

26

YOU'RE ONLY AS SICK
AS YOUR SECRETS

The old Chevy Malibu sat parked at the far reaches of the parking lot. Two faded and peeling bumper stickers adorned the rust-mottled bumper. *Easy Does It.* And *Let Go and Let God.*

There were two women in the car. Dressed for comfort in a white nylon jogging suit, Martha sat behind the wheel and watched the entrance of the Shoney's restaurant through a pair of binoculars. These weren't ordinary binoculars. Martha had paid a considerable amount for them. These were Zeiss FL Victory with Water Proof Roof Prism. The binoculars had an 8.0-degree angle of view. The catalog stated that the Zeiss was ideally suited for stalking and field ornithology. There were no birds out tonight.

"But you've only been sober six months now. It's not a contest, dear. Besides, for many of us, the ninth step is the hardest one. The eighth and the ninth go hand in hand. Make a list of all the people you've harmed and then make amends to those people wherever possible."

"I'm stuck on the last item on my list," Helen said.

"The drunk driving accident."

Martha sat up a little straighter and focused the binoculars. A little potbellied balding man and a teenage boy exited the restaurant. From Martha's body language, Helen could tell that these were the ones Martha had been waiting on. They looked like any typical father and son to Helen. Out for their big night at Shoney's. They climbed into a white Chevrolet Equinox and drove away. Martha started her Malibu and followed.

"The accident. The hit-and-run," Helen said. "And are you ready to tell me what exactly we are doing?"

"I'll explain later. I want to know what's eating at you."

Helen frowned. "I want to work the steps. And I want to work them right. I don't know how to make amends."

"Well, what's the problem, dear? So you bent somebody's fender. Admit it to them. Pay for the repair work. Tell them you're sorry. You will be shocked at how forgiving people can be when you're forthright with them. When you are truly trying to make amends."

Helen didn't respond.

"You're making too big a deal out of it. Building it up in your mind. It's not like you killed someone."

Still, Helen remained silent. She would not look at Martha.

"You left something out, didn't you? When you unburdened yourself to me. The fifth step."

Helen nodded her head.

"It doesn't have to be me, you know. You could tell it to a priest. Or a shrink. Or a complete stranger. But you have to admit to another human being the exact nature of your wrongs. You can't cheat the steps."

Helen said, by rote, "You gotta work it if you want it to work."

"I've taught you well, Grasshopper."

They drove in silence for a while longer, each of them thinking.

"Maybe, dear, it's better if I'm not the one you tell. Maybe . . . Well, the point is, you have to do it. You have to admit to another human being the exact nature of your wrongs. I'm not trying to be cruel. The point is that this thing, whatever it is, will prey on your mind."

"'You're only as sick as your secrets.' I know."

"You're putting your sobriety at risk. You have—"

"I did, Martha."

"You did what?"

"I did kill someone."

Martha turned her head and stared at Helen, her mouth hanging open. She slammed on the brakes when she almost rear-ended the car she had been following.

"Jesus."

27

THE DIRTY LITTLE THINGS
WE DO TO ONE ANOTHER

Martha's car was in the parking lot of the liquor store where Helen had bought her last bottle of vodka—the radiation-free kind.

The two women leaned against the Malibu with its blistered paint and rust-flecked body. Helen told Martha everything. The whole story. The crime, the cover-up, and how the guilt was blooming inside her like toxic black mold. Helen smoked a cigarette and waited for Martha to respond, but Martha only peered through her binoculars, watching the man from the restaurant walk into the front office of a hotel, a three-level motor court directly across the four-lane.

Martha put the binoculars on the hood of the car and took hold of Helen's hand.

"I had to tell my brother that I knew, had known all my life, that our father had been molesting him. And I did nothing to stop it. That was my ninth step. I knew about it and kept quiet. Because I was afraid.

"I was afraid that our father would come after me. That he would come to my bed. Or worse, that my father would hate me for telling on him. I loved him. I was his princess. So I had to tell my brother that I could have stopped years of his abuse, but didn't.

"Derek's been treated for mental illness most of his adult life. Spent time in jail. And his problems almost certainly stemmed from that abuse. So yes, that was my ninth step. Owning that. How do you make amends for something like that? You can't. There was nothing that I could actually do to repair the damage I caused. And I had to ask myself if confessing to him would only cause him more pain. We must never unburden ourselves if sharing that knowledge only hurts the other person. If we are only transferring that burden from ourselves to them. In the end, I decided that my admission would give him some kind of validation. Our father never admitted the abuse. So I told him. And it almost killed me. But I did it. And he forgave me. He forgave me, dear. He said that he had felt guilty all of those years. That he thought that I thought the abuse was his fault. That I blamed him for destroying our family."

Martha retrieved the binoculars and watched the man get back in his car and drive deeper into the motor court parking lot.

"I did it. I made amends. And it worked. If you want it to work, you gotta work the steps. I haven't had a drink in fourteen years. I've done a lot of shitty, despicable things in my life. But my conscience is clear. I'm a good person."

It was such a painful story that Helen had to look away from Martha. She said, "I had an uncle. He was supposed to be teaching me to swim. But he . . . he, uh, he would hold me in the water. And he would . . ."

"I think I get the picture."

"He would hold my head under the water if I didn't do what he wanted."

"Jesus wept."

Martha watched the man and the boy climb the concrete stairs to the third level of the hotel.

"I told my mother. But she didn't believe me. Uncle Billy was her brother, so she didn't believe me. She couldn't allow herself to believe that about her oldest brother. She kept dropping me off at his house for swimming lessons. Validation. She never believed me. So yes, validation would mean everything. You gave your brother a gift."

"In a way. Yes. The dirty little things we do to one another."

"I don't swim. To this day I'm afraid of the water."

"I imagine so."

The man and the boy reached the open balcony of the third level. Martha reached into her backseat and pulled out a sophisticated electronic camera with an imposing telephoto lens.

Helen stared at Martha and gestured at the camera, ready for an explanation.

"I work for an investigator. It's cheaters mostly."

The camera clicked and whirred as Martha worked it.

"The dirty little things we do to one another."

28

DO NO HARM

Once the hotel room door was closed, Martha put the camera back in the car.

"The question," Helen said, "is how do you make amends for taking someone's life?"

"Maybe, dear, you don't. You're willing to make amends, that's clear; that's step eight. But step nine, it says, 'made direct amends to such people wherever possible, except when to do so would injure them or others.'"

Martha took Helen's hand and squeezed it firmly. "'Except when to do so would injure them or others.'"

"I could turn myself in to the police."

"That's true dear, you could. And you would probably go to jail. And your conscience would be clear. But what about your little vet clinic? I suppose it would close. And the people who work for you? I suppose they would be unemployed. And the animals you shelter? Euthanized, I imagine. You might feel less guilty, but the people and things that depend on you . . ."

"It feels wrong."

"In the end, nothing you do will bring that poor woman back. She's beyond your help. Ultimately, what we are talking about is you—your sobriety. And honestly, I can't think of anything you could do that wouldn't hurt you or others. You've admitted it. You've owned it. Ask God for forgiveness. Do good things in your life. And don't pick up a drink."

"I can't bring her back, you're right. But what about the man whose wife I took away? I should make amends to him. He's the one I should—"

"Stop and think. Just stop and think. Will that help or hurt this person? Will knowing who is responsible help or hurt him? He's likely made his own peace with what happened. If you approach him, that could very well disturb his mind. You do not ease your own burden by transferring it to others to carry. That strikes to the very heart of the ninth step. First, do no harm. If you entered this man's life, would it help or hurt him?"

"I just don't know."

"Then find out, dear. Before you go messing around in people's lives, find out. Or take my advice and simply leave it alone."

29

GOING ON SEVEN MONTHS NOW

Edgar sat at his desk between the foyer and the living room. Directly behind him was the glass display case that held his puzzle box collection. Most of the puzzles that weren't traditional Japanese boxes had come from Judy as gifts over the years. She had never been able to find one he couldn't solve. But it was fun trying.

Edgar's desk was a marvel of organization. Nothing out of place. And a sleek black computer sat antiseptically on top. He took a stack of flyers from his leather satchel and placed them in the filing cabinet. They were leftovers. He had spent the day placing them under the wiper blades of cars parked at local businesses. The handbills were simple things—stating the date, time, and location of the accident, along with Edgar's name, phone number, e-mail, and street address. *Please, if you have any information, no matter how small, contact me.*

Next, he went to work on a stack of mail, methodically opening each envelope, slitting it neatly with a silver letter opener. Should any bits of paper or dust fall onto the desktop during this process, he would promptly scoop the offending mess into a small trash can.

Most of the mail was bills. He promptly paid these online. No convenience of fully automated payments in the Woolrich household. And he insisted on hard copies of all statements. Edgar felt it best to review each bill in both its printed and electronic formats before clicking the "transfer funds" button. Like many who were not born into the online generation, Edgar relied on the Internet, yet harbored a vestigial distrust of it, particularly when it came to matters of finance. So he exercised caution. Kept a close watch. The road to hell, he believed, was likely paved with autopay errors.

The remainder of the stack consisted mostly of advertisements. One was a piece of junk mail addressed to Judy Woolrich. It was going on seven months now and still she got mail. Edgar opened it and retrieved the reply envelope from inside. He then opened his file drawer and extracted a form letter—of which he had printed twenty copies. It read: *Mrs. Judy Woolrich is deceased. Please remove her name from your database.*

Edgar signed the letter, folded it into a razor-edged triptych, and sealed it in the envelope.

After that, he got up and went to the kitchen, where he placed one of Jane's frozen dinners in the microwave and set it to cook for ten minutes.

Back at his desk, he looked up at the state map that was mounted to the wall there. Neatly drawn concentric circles rippled out from the area of origination—which was labeled *Crash Site*. Each circle was dotted with numbers and letters. The numbers corresponded with car dealerships, the letters to automotive repair shops.

A wall chart was mounted directly next to the state map. This chart was labeled *CHAOS AND CRIME BIFURCATION MAP*. The chart was a complex series of egg-shaped swoops and swirls. The legend at the bottom neatly indicated that the solid lines represented stable crime statistics, while the dotted line represented chaos.

Edgar affixed a blank chart to the wall and, using a Sharpie marker, labeled it *LIKELIHOODS*. He wrote:

# of cars of any color on road in 2-hour time frame
Number of red cars in that period
Prevalence of red cars on road in that time period
Percentage of all cars that are red
Percentage of red cars on road during given time frame
Mean difference
Chance of being struck by a red car—on that road—during that time frame

Next Edgar performed a quick Google search for the term "percent red cars road" and navigated to a web page with a bar graph that listed vehicle color popularity. The color red was graphed at 7 percent. Edgar clicked the "print" button, and a copy of the graph whispered from his laser printer. He added the printout to a bulging file labeled *Statistics*. He made a mental note to split the file into parts A and B so that it wouldn't bulge so much.

Referencing his notes from late-night car counting, Edgar began to fill in the new wall chart. The doorbell rang, and Edgar capped the marker.

30

NOTE TO SELF

Parked at the curb, Helen sat in her car and watched Edgar's house. The blinds were down and the curtains were drawn, showing only a bit of yellowish light behind them—like embers banked in deep ash.

Helen unfolded her clenched fist to reveal her six-month so-briety chip. In actuality, it was a blue poker chip available by the gross at Walmarts across the world. To her, it was everything. She placed it on the dashboard of her car and went to the front door.

Although she had parked on this street and watched this house in the past, she had never actually seen Edgar Woolrich up close. The man who opened the door squinted at her behind ludicrously thick bifocals. He looked to Helen like a mole. An inquisitive mole.

She found that she couldn't speak. She couldn't introduce herself to this man. Blood flushed the capillaries of her face as all of her resolve drained away.

"May I help you?" he asked, when it became clear that Helen was not going to voluntarily explain her presence.

Helen opened her mouth and was surprised to hear words come out of it.

"I've come about your wife."

Helen couldn't understand Edgar's initial reaction to her presence. He smiled. The man had smiled and invited her in. He acted almost as though he expected her. As though he considered it normal for a stranger to show up on his doorstep late in the evening inquiring about his dead wife. He'd said, "I almost didn't put my address on it. Most people do e-mail or a phone call. But I wanted to be thorough." Then a beeping sound diverted his attention and he excused himself to the kitchen.

She stared at the maps, charts, and graphs on Edgar's walls. Much of it she didn't understand, but the gist was quite obvious. The man was not at peace. He was carrying a burden. He wanted to find the person responsible for killing his wife. Helen clenched her fist, wishing she had brought the chip with her.

"They help me to keep things straight in my mind," Edgar said, back from the kitchen, a box of colored Sharpies in one hand and a steaming green Tupperware container in the other.

"This is so . . . thorough."

"She was pregnant, did you know that?"

"No. I'm so sorry."

Edgar placed his dinner on the corner of his work desk, using a hot pad to protect the wood surface. He pulled a ledger from one of the drawers and flipped through it. "Give me just a minute. I want to update a color code for this."

Helen's attention was drawn to the glass-enclosed case on the far wall. She crossed over to it and took in the display. At first, she thought they were objects of art, but she quickly realized that they were puzzles of some kind. There was a plain-looking wooden box—no bigger than her fist—alongside which stood a neatly printed card informing the observer that this was a seventy-eight-step nineteenth-century Japanese puzzle box, *himitsu-bako*.

Helen opened the case and carefully picked up the box. She was surprised at how light it was. She quickly replaced it, careful to position it exactly as she had found it. When she was finished, she found that Edgar was standing directly behind her. He reached into the case and repositioned the box. To Helen, it looked as though he had changed its position by, maybe, a millimeter. She thought, *Note to self: Do not touch the puzzle boxes.*

"Have you ever done a Rubik's Cube?" she asked.

"That's not really where my interest lies."

"Oh. But have you ever done one? I had one in seventh grade. I never did solve it."

"Really?" His tone was deadpan.

"Really. So, have you?"

One eyebrow arched up over the top of his glasses, as he looked at her in question.

"Done a Rubik's Cube. Have you?"

"Mass-produced games and puzzles hold little interest for me."

"So the answer is no."

"Correct. The answer is no," Edgar replied, conceding the point.

"You should buy one. If anyone could solve one of those, it's you."

"I really don't think it would hold much—" Edgar cut himself off. From the look on his face, it was clear to Helen he was irritated to have allowed himself to be drawn into this particular conversation. Edgar sat down and cracked open the ledger. "How did I first contact you? Was it the flyer? An e-mail? Do you work in the area? Or are you a resident? I'll need to plot it."

Helen was lost. She looked from the maps to the charts, to the puzzle boxes, and finally to the open, hopeful look in Edgar's eyes. She didn't know what to say.

"I don't mean to be overly personal. It will help me to know how I intersected with you. So that I expand the area of probability. You see?"

Helen most certainly did not see. But she was able to piece together that Edgar was investigating his wife's death, and he thought that Helen was here in response to some flyer or phone call he had made.

"Do you have something for me? Information?"

Helen felt blindsided. The moment had rushed up on her.

She thought she would have had the chance to feel him out a little and work her way up to this moment. But the moment was here. And there was no equivocation. There was no room for doubt or debate. The man wanted to know. It was a puzzle he could not solve, and he would find no peace until he solved it. It was clear. Now was the time. This was it.

"Yes," Helen said. Edgar leaned forward, pen poised over the ledger. "I mean no. I mean . . . I was there. That night. I drove past. After. I didn't stop. I didn't stop and I felt so bad that I didn't stop and I just—"

"You're here because you feel bad because you didn't stop? After the accident had occurred?"

Helen nodded, on the brink of tears, ashamed of both her secret and the lie she had just told. What had happened to her courage? To her resolve?

Edgar reached out, as though to touch her, to comfort her, but then withdrew his hand.

"No. It doesn't matter. You couldn't have done anything. She was dead within minutes. She was . . . You couldn't have helped. You have nothing to feel guilty about. Nothing. Were there other vehicles around? Did you see anybody else? The other car?"

Helen shook her head.

"Nothing. The ambulance was about half a mile behind me. I'm . . . I'm an—"

Edgar nodded and held his hand out in such a way that it communicated to Helen that he was absolving her and at the same time had lost interest in her. He was ready for her to go. He walked toward her, his hand rising to usher her toward the door.

"I can help you," Helen offered. She didn't want the encounter to end. Not like this. Not with the lie still on her lips. "I can talk to people. I can help look. I can—"

"That won't be necessary. Thank you for coming."

He had corralled her so quickly that she just had time to realize that she was once again standing on the front porch when the door closed quietly in her face.

YOU HAVE THREE SECONDS
TO VACATE

The front door opened and the woman walked back inside his home.

"No," she said, "I can't leave yet."

Edgar was appalled. It was bad enough that she had come here seeking only solace for herself; now she was an actual intruder. Some of his puzzle boxes were of genuine value. For all he knew, her goal could be to divert his attention and steal a handful of them.

"You can't leave yet? Of course you can leave. Just turn around."

"No. I'm . . . I . . . I have to help you. I want to help you."

"I don't want your help. I want you to leave. Are you unstable?"

"Un . . . ? What? Look, you're trying to accomplish something here. And you're alone. You're alone and . . . and you don't have to be. What if I helped make calls or something?"

"Make calls? I want you to leave my house and take your help with you. I don't need it."

"What if—"

"No."

"Maybe I—"

"No."

The woman—she'd never introduced herself, so he would have no name to give to the police should it come to that—lowered her head and pinched the bridge of her nose. When she raised her head and looked up at him, he saw anger in her eyes. They were like cold marble. And then he realized that it wasn't anger he saw in those eyes. It was something like anguish. Or was it pity?

"You need help."

"Excuse me?"

"You need help. I need to help someone. See how that evens out?"

"Equations. Those I can understand. Unfortunately, your hypothesis is wrong. Why would you think I need help? And if I did, why would I accept it from a total stranger?"

"Because it's what you need." She indicated the wall charts, the ledger. "This, this, this. Not healthy."

"True. It's probably not. But it's really none of your business. And why do you *need* to help someone?"

"It's not that I need to. It's, well, I'm in recovery. In a program. And anything that you feel bad about, that worries you, nags at you, you have to address it, take care of it."

"I told you, there was nothing you could have done. And you said the ambulance was right behind you anyway. I forgive you. Now please leave."

"Let me help you."

"I asked you to leave."

The woman crossed her arms and just stood there. Edgar picked up the telephone. He made an elaborate show of dialing 9 and 1—leaving his thumb poised over the final 1.

"You have three seconds to vacate."

The woman's hands rose in a warding-off gesture, and she slowly backed out the door.

32

FULL OF POTENTIAL

Edgar held his crisply folded sack lunch in one hand and a thick book in the other. There was something about walking down a school hallway when it was empty between classes. It seemed so full of potential.

The illusion of solitude was spoiled. Up ahead, he saw four boys scuffling around an open locker. As he drew closer, Edgar saw Jack Mendelson and two of his cronies. They all wore denim clothes and leather work boots. Standard issue. As usual, Martin Kosinski was at the center of it all. They saw Edgar coming and pushed Martin into the nearby boys' bathroom.

Edgar paused at the bathroom door. He could hear muffled taunts. Edgar looked at the book in his right hand. *Crime and Chaos Theory*. There was a time that he believed his interventions could save Martin. But not now. Not now.

33

RIGID ANGLES AND
BRIGHT PRIMARY COLORS

Surrounded by his charts, graphs, equations, and bifurcation maps, Edgar sat in his living room on Saturday afternoon, reading. There was no sound other than the faint humming of the refrigerator compressor—punctuated with the occasional dropping of ice cubes from the ice maker.

He was using five highlighters of differing colors to carefully mark passages he found of particular importance. Chaos and crime was an emerging science, and comparatively very little had been written about it. It consumed his waking hours. Even Edgar was aware that it had become an obsession. Not healthy, he'd been recently told.

He uncapped the red pen and highlighted a passage: *It takes but a small change in everyday factors to bring about victimization.*

The victim may desire to not be a victim. Remember, chaos cannot be predicted, but it can be controlled to an extent.

Edgar heard a vehicle outside. He had ordered a new textbook from a publisher in the United Kingdom and was eager to receive it. It had been quite expensive, and Edgar was afraid that he would have to sell one of his better puzzle boxes on eBay to cover his bills. He peeked through the curtain, hoping to see the familiar brown color of UPS, but instead saw a black Honda Insight. It was that woman.

Edgar watched her emerge from her car carrying a casserole dish and head for the front steps. He crossed over to the front door and opened it before she could ring the bell. Edgar looked the woman in the eye, calmly shook his head no, and closed the door in her face.

At suppertime, Edgar decided to go pick up something from a fast-food drive-through. He opened his front door and found the casserole dish sitting on the top step. He stepped over it and continued on his way.

The next day, upon arriving home from the grocery store, Edgar found that the casserole and dish had been replaced with a fresh one. He stepped over it and continued on into his house.

After school on Monday, he found yet another casserole dish awaiting him. He picked it up and considered it a moment. He then hurtled it out into the street, where it smashed.

To the empty street he yelled, "Leave me alone!"

He would have to clean up the mess himself, but for now, for the moment, the violent gesture brought him comfort. After that, Edgar took to picking up the casserole dishes and promptly dropping them in the trash. He figured that at some point the constant replacement of the dishes might become too much of a financial burden for the woman.

Late the following week, Edgar pulled one of Jane's homemade TV dinners out of the freezer. It was frost-burned and looked not at all appealing, but he had neglected to shop for groceries, and he just didn't feel up to the drive-through yet again.

The microwave got it too hot and the Tupperware warped. He used a hot pad to carry it to his desk so he could eat while he worked.

From outside, Edgar could hear a car door close and the car pull away. He opened his front door and found the usual casserole dish on the top step. The sight of it made him angry. He picked it up, reared back to sling it into the street, but then looked back over his shoulder at the meal he was about to eat. Pale turkey in scorched gravy next to discolored peas. The whole thing held in a plastic container melted into a scallop shape and leaching God knew what kind of chemicals into the food.

Edgar peeked under the casserole dish's lid. Some kind of spaghetti concoction. Cheese melted to a crispy gold crusted the top. It looked pretty damn good. Edgar swept his eyes covertly side to side—as though making sure he wasn't being observed in the commission of a felonious act—and took the casserole inside.

* * *

Day after day Edgar found different goodies waiting for him on his front step. He realized what a snobbish fool he'd been to refuse the earlier offers. If the woman felt compelled to do him some good service, then who was he to deny her that opportunity? He reasoned that she wasn't actually trying to do something for him so much as she wanted to ease her own guilty conscience. By accepting the food, he was the one who was helping her.

Without realizing it, Edgar had undergone, quite literally, the same conditioning as Pavlov's dogs. He now watched the clock every day, waiting on the delivery of his own personal Meals on Wheels. He always waited until six o'clock before opening the door, and, although he was quite unaware of it, his digestive juices started flowing about five minutes before that. And those juices were invariably rewarded for their Boy Scout–like preparedness.

He never saw the woman. And for that he was grateful. Grateful for the cushion afforded by the lack of familiarity. From five thirty until six o'clock he found things upstairs to occupy his time. Although he was sometimes tempted to peek through the curtain and observe the delivery, he was more inclined to preserve the fabrication of anonymity.

One day, a small, colorfully wrapped, cube-shaped object accompanied the meal. A small card taped to it said: *If anybody can do it . . . Helen.*

Helen. So that was her name. So much for anonymity, fabricated or not.

Of course Edgar immediately guessed what would be under the wrapping. It was a Rubik's Cube. Apparently, it was not even a new one. There was no packaging and the colors were already scrambled. He shook his head the way an adult does when a child makes a rude remark in utter innocence. Edgar had thus far avoided Mr. Rubik's wildly popular little conundrum. He had always preferred boxes and puzzles that held a secret locked away inside them. A hidden compartment or drawer. The joy for Edgar did not lie so much in the solving, but in the discovery of the secret.

After he had eaten his dinner (fried catfish with coleslaw and homemade hush puppies—the meals had evolved from simple casseroles), Edgar nonetheless found himself drawn to the cube. It was a puzzle, and he was Edgar. Puzzles needed solving whether there was something inside them or not.

He picked the thing up and, frowning in concentration, began twisting it. Soon, he was lost in its rigid angles and bright primary colors.

34

PROBABLY DRUNK WHEN SHE DID IT

It was five till six and Edgar sat on the edge of his bed fidgeting with the accursed cube. He hated the damn thing. It was unsolvable. He had begun to wonder if the woman, Helen High and Mighty, had sabotaged it somehow to get back at him for his puzzle snobbery. The colors on the surface were just plastic stickers. She could have easily peeled and reglued a couple of them in the wrong place. Probably drunk when she did it. Hadn't she said something about being in recovery?

His stomach told him that it was now at least a few minutes after six. His dinner should be there, waiting on him. Edgar set the cube down and headed downstairs to the front door. He paused in the living room and fixed one of his charts—one corner had come loose from the wall and drooped over like a dog's ear. He assessed all of the charts for a moment. They had not changed much in the last several weeks. It wasn't that he had lost interest, he didn't think. It was that his mind seemed to be growing cloudy, almost befuddled. The Rubik's Cube was case in point. If he couldn't figure out a little brainteaser that schoolchildren—schoolchildren, for God's sake—could solve in a matter of seconds, then how was he going to wrap his mind around chaos theory?

His appetite, however, was fine. Edgar opened the front door. His dinner was not sitting on the front step. His dinner was cradled in the arms of the woman, Helen.

They stared at each other for a moment, neither knowing the appropriate words to speak. Or perhaps they both knew it was better to not speak at all.

After a while, Edgar took the dish from Helen's arms and motioned her inside.

35

HELEN KELLER'S HAND

Helen sat with Edgar on the wooden bench in the waiting area of the detective bureau. Edgar was holding large rectangles of poster board in his lap. They were multicolored bifurcation maps with areas clearly labeled *CERTAINTY*, *PREDICTION*, and *CONTROL*.

To Helen, Edgar looked exactly like a little boy waiting for his big moment at the elementary school science fair. She supposed that would make her the doting, overprotective mother.

It had been three months since he invited her inside to eat with him. She was just trying to be his friend. She didn't know what else to do. He was so intensely alone. At the same time, Helen was very much aware that she had befriended a man whose sole goal in life was to find the person who was responsible for taking Judy Woolrich's life. And that person was sitting right beside him. That person had been eating dinner with him twice a week for the last twelve weeks. In a very real way, Helen realized, it was cruel. But she had come to further realize that any revelation on her part would not fix what was broken in this man. And he was now her responsibility. Fixing the broken part was her responsibility.

So, when he was called over to the detective's desk, Helen (the hit-and-run driver that they were all looking for) watched Edgar make his way over to the detectives.

Edgar handed the first detective the bifurcation maps. The detective, a tall woman whom he had said was named Poole, took the charts and seemed to give them serious consideration. Helen could see Edgar pointing out aspects of them, trying to impart importance. After a few moments, Detective Poole folded the charts and slid them under Edgar's arm. She talked to Edgar for a while, using her hands to make her points. Edgar unfolded the charts and pointed something out, and Helen already knew him well enough to know that he was frustrated that he had been unable to convey the possibilities hidden there.

She felt a sharp iciness in her spine when Detective Poole turned away from Edgar and looked directly at Helen. Edgar turned to follow the detective's gaze, and then both of them were looking straight at Helen. Still staring directly at Helen, the detective said something to Edgar, and then they both looked away.

* * *

Edgar tossed his charts into the backseat, clearly unhappy with Detective Poole's dismissal of their importance. Helen slid into the passenger seat. She watched Edgar climb in, sorry for his disappointment but also concerned that she had been a topic of discussion.

"What did she say to you?"

"She said that the case was dead. Not closed, because they don't close unsolved homicides. But it's inactive. That I should let it go."

"I'm sorry."

"Me too."

"Maybe she's—"

"Don't."

"But when she looked at me. When you both looked at me, she said something."

"I don't remember."

"You don't remember? It was thirty seconds ago."

"It wasn't anything important."

"Bullshit."

"Why do you want to know so bad?" It was an accusation.

"You're right. It's none of my business. I'm sorry."

"No, I'm sorry. I'm being stupid. It hurt. What she said made me hurt. So stupid."

"What?"

"It's just that she saw you sitting there waiting for me."

"So?"

"So, I've never gone there with anybody before."

"Oh. Okay. I think I get it."

"All she said was: 'It looks like you've got a friend now. Go with that.'"

"Are you ashamed to have a friend?"

Edgar shook his head.

"Guilty?"

Edgar's silence confirmed rather than denied. Helen reached out to put a soothing hand on his cheek, but Edgar pulled away. He looked at her, and she saw the regret in his eyes. He reached out his own hand and lightly brushed her cheek. Without giving Edgar time to think or respond, Helen darted her head in and planted a chaste kiss on his dry lips.

"Start the car. Let's go grocery shopping. I want to cook you dinner."

Edgar pushed the cart, and Helen tossed fresh carrots, celery, parsley, and onions into it. She found a nice crusty French bread and threw that in as well. She grabbed some cheese, a box of crackers, tea, and other things she thought Edgar should keep on hand. At the butcher counter she found a fat chicken to boil for soup. When she went to place it in the cart, she found that Edgar had arranged all the food in a compact, interlocked design. He saw the look on her face and said, "You don't have to worry about it shifting out of place."

"You're kidding, right? Please say you're kidding."

Edgar shrugged.

"Look, let go and let—I mean, damn, Edgar, just let go."

Helen reached into the shopping cart and shoved the food items into disarray. She messed up all of the order, all of the Edgarness.

Edgar frowned at the lack of purpose strewn before him. He took the plastic-wrapped chicken from Helen, considered it a moment, and then dropped it into the cart with what he thought was nonchalance, but to Helen looked more akin to an agoraphobe contemplating a stadium full of people.

Helen said, "I feel like Annie Sullivan running water over Helen Keller's hand."

Edgar grinned. Then started to chuckle at himself. Soon it was genuine laughter, full and real.

36

WHAT IF HE FINDS OUT?

It wasn't Smitty's Cocktails, but it was still a bar. Martha and Helen were sequestered in a dim booth to the rear. Helen had protested at the idea of going to a bar, but Martha simply said that it had been a long day and she could use a drink.

When Helen didn't smile, Martha said, "Sorry, dear, old AA joke. They say you should avoid bars like the plague. They trigger drinking memories. Well, I like to feel comfortable. And where do drunks feel most comfortable? Whistle past the graveyard, I say."

"Sometimes I wonder if you're truly sponsor material."

"I wonder that myself."

"I've told you some pretty damning things, you know?"

"I do know. And I know what you're about to ask me. So just get it out there."

"The things I've told you. I mean, I've told you—"

The waitress appeared and tossed two cocktail napkins on the table like she was dealing a quick hand of blackjack. She propped her little cork-lined serving tray on her hip and cocked an eyebrow at her newest customers. That eyebrow seemed to say, *I've pegged you two for nontippers, but I'm going to take your order anyway, so let's have it.*

Martha pulled a twenty out of her purse and laid it on the table. "Two club sodas." The waitress meandered away in the general direction of the bar. "Club soda work for you?"

Helen nodded.

"All right. Down to business. What you told me, you told me in the confines of our AA relationship. I'm your sponsor. Anything you tell me in that regard is legally considered privileged information. The same as if I were your doctor, lawyer, or God forbid, priest."

"You're all three."

"Meh."

"I've been trying to make his life better. That's my amends to him."

"But . . ."

"But it feels like maybe I'm doing something wrong."

"It *is* wrong, dear. It *is* wrong."

"But you would never tell. You could never tell."

Martha opened her purse and pulled out a book. *Twelve Steps and Twelve Traditions.* It was well used, and the word *surrender* was scratched in ink along the top edges.

"I've been thinking about you. About your dilemma. And I wanted to read this to you. It concerns step nine. 'We cannot buy our own peace of mind at the expense of others.'"

Martha laid the book down on top of the twenty-dollar bill.

"Do you understand what that means? I'm sure that what you're doing for this man is making *you* feel better. It's buying your own peace of mind. And right now I suppose it's even helping him. But what if he finds out, dear? What if he finds out that he's befriended the woman—"

The waitress rested her hip against the booth like a long-distance swimmer finally reaching shore. She sat down the club sodas on the previously placed napkins. Martha slid the money from under the *Twelve Steps* book, tucked it in the waitress's change apron, and, with a wink, told her to keep the change. Clearly caught off guard by the unexpected generosity, the woman mumbled a word of thanks.

"I used to wait tables myself. I know what it's like." She turned back to Helen and said, "I've always believed in rewarding good service."

"It took her ten minutes to fetch two club sodas. And there's no ice in them. And on top of that, you hardly rewarded her. Looked to me like you left her owing the till about eight dollars."

"I'm sorry, dear, I'm not following. What are you saying?"

Helen stared her down.

"What?"

"You just gave that woman a dollar bill and told her it was a twenty."

"I did no such thing."

"Martha, I saw."

"No, I'm quite certain it was a twenty. I remember pulling it—"

Helen shook her head.

"Are you sure, dear?"

Helen leaned across the table and picked up the *Twelve Steps* book. There, underneath, lay the twenty-dollar bill.

"Well, I never told her it was a twenty. She just assumed." Martha sighed, her eyes clouding over with nostalgia. "I really shouldn't come into bars. It *does* bring back old habits. I used to be something of a . . . In my drinking days, we used to . . . I guess I just wanted to see if I could still do it. We all have a past, dear. Mine's as black as yours. And believe me, I never went back and repaid every few dollars I grifted off someone. That would have been impossible. And stupid."

"You wanted me to see that."

"Maybe I did. The point is: You can have done bad things but still be a good person. I have, and I am. A good person."

Martha took the twenty and tucked it under her glass.

"No harm, no foul. If you can make amends, then make amends. Just be damn sure you don't do more harm than good."

"I want to make his happiness my job."

"Your job is staying sober. One day—"

"At a time. I get it. And helping him helps keep me from picking up a drink."

"Just be careful. Let go—"

"And let God. We need some fresher expressions."

Martha extended her clenched hand across the table.

"Fist bump."

Helen reciprocated, and the two women knocked knuckles.

"Blow it up."

37

HE COULD QUITE POSSIBLY HIT HER

Edgar slept.

Sprawled in his recliner, he slept deeply, the still unsolved Rubik's Cube resting squarely on his chest. He dreamed of Judy. Awake, even after all this time, he never allowed himself the momentary lapses of memory that many a grieving spouse sometimes indulged in. He never forgot, not for the briefest of lapses, that Judy was dead. But when he dreamed, Judy was alive, and the notion of her death was unfathomable.

Helen knelt beside him, her head resting in his lap, her hand stroking his leg.

Her hand crept higher and higher, seeking a sexual response. Edgar's body responded.

Edgar groaned in his sleep, stretching with pleasure.

Helen stood, leaned over Edgar, and kissed him. Her hand was still in his lap. She took the unsolved cube off his chest and placed it on the floor. "Told you," she whispered and smiled.

Helen unbuckled his belt, freed him from the underwear. She pulled down her own pants and stepped out of them. She straddled Edgar in the chair, drawing him into her.

After a while, the whole of Edgar's body responded, thrusting into her, matching her rhythm. He was awakening. He mumbled "No," even as his body responded to the sex act. He pulled Helen down to him and kissed her with a fervor of which she would have thought him incapable. He rose up and flipped them both so that he was in charge of the act. Helen decided to be whatever he needed her to be, to do whatever he needed her to do.

In the morning, Helen woke up in Edgar's bed. When she opened her eyes, she could tell that Edgar was awake as well. She could sense his thoughts. She found it hard to make initial eye contact with him and sensed that he, likewise, did not want to look into her eyes, fearful of what he might silently communicate to her. Of course she would have to look at him at some point, so she did it now, saying "Good morning" and casting her eyes upward. She was surprised that the guilt feeling was not there—not on her part, or his. She saw no guilt or shame in his eyes.

Helen scooted out of bed and went down the hall to the bathroom. At the end of the hallway, a closed door caught her eye. She had never been upstairs before. All the other doors in the house were kept open. She opened the door. Inside, she found a nursery. An infant's bedroom that had never been used. Many of the items were still packaged and shrink-wrapped.

She poked the mobile that was suspended over the crib, setting it in motion. She sensed something behind her and found Edgar watching her from the doorway. Now, she felt guilty.

"Judy had this room ready three years before she got pregnant. She never doubted that we would be able to make a baby. And she was right."

Helen stopped the mobile. She spoke so lightly that her voice could barely be heard, but what she said was intended to provoke him: "You have to move on."

"What?"

"I said you have to move on."

Like a roulette wheel, she watched different emotions flicker over Edgar's face, finally settling on anger.

Rage contorted his features. "How dare you?"

Helen stuck with the script that she had come up with. She sensed that to turn back would be a bigger risk than pushing forward. She went to him, stood inches away from him, and the thought that he could quite possibly hit her flitted through her mind. She reached up and pulled his face to hers. "You have to move on."

A choked sob escaped from Edgar. She pulled him in closer. Held him. And it worked. All the poison came out. No, she had not seen guilt in his eyes this morning. It had been buried too deep for that.

When Edgar broke the bond, he looked at Helen and asked, "Is this real?"

"It's real."

And she knew that standing here with a woman in his never-born child's room did not feel real to Edgar. But she knew that she could make it real.

38

AN OMEN

Tyler Ketchum ran through the green grass waving a Fourth of July sparkler. His little sister, Savannah, chased after him as best she could. Mitzi loped behind, not wanting to get too close to the burning sulfur smell.

It was a barbecue in Edgar's backyard. Because of the pool, a privacy fence encircled the property. In addition to that, the old neighborhood had stands of mature maples and banks of pin oaks hemming in the houses. Well-established arbors, towering stands of leggy nandinas, and an undeveloped woodlot gave the backyard total privacy.

From the kitchen window, Helen watched the children running through the yard while she rinsed vegetables in the sink for a dip tray. She could also see Jane and Steve Ketchum, who were reclining poolside, watching Elmore do tricks off the diving board. It had felt odd meeting them—intensely uncomfortable was more accurate—but Edgar had his heart set on it. Helen looked around for Edgar but didn't see him outside anywhere.

Helen looked different somehow. It could have been that her hair was different—she was wearing it a bit shorter. It could have been that she was just feeling more relaxed in her own skin these days. Or perhaps it was nothing more than the simple beauty of the summery drop-waist dress she was wearing.

Edgar sneaked up on her and nuzzled her from behind. She swatted him away, feigning annoyance, but Edgar persisted, running his hands over the front of her dress, gently cupping her breasts. Then his hands trailed lower before disappearing under the hemline of her dress. Helen squirmed and giggled, turning to face him. She squealed as Edgar lifted her onto the sink and took a deep breath as she saw the direction his head was moving in. With a nervous glance out the window, she opened herself to him.

"Oh, Edgar, you're so—thorough."

It was the first time Edgar had opened the pool this summer. Spring rains had collected on the heavy plastic cover and eventually pulled it loose from the side moorings—so insects and debris had accumulated for quite some time. It had taken a full day to clean out the trash and then filter and chemically treat the water.

Helen's records clerk, Kelly, unscrewed the top off a Rolling

Rock and watched Elmore climb the three risers to the diving board. (While she was working her steps, Helen had gone to Elmore, asked his forgiveness, and offered him his job back.) Not shy, Elmore took three heavy, purposeful steps on the plank, and his massive girth bent the diving board so that the tip actually touched the water. The board sprang back and rocketed him high in the air. He tucked in his knees, held them tight with clasped hands, and came down in a perfectly executed cannonball. *Thuwhuuuump!* The splash was like a depth charge. Jane, who had just had her hair done and had no intention of getting it wet today, screamed and yelled, "Goddamn it!" Her husband, Steve, suppressed a smile, secretly delighted.

Elmore bobbed to the surface and spotted Helen and Edgar emerging from the house carrying food trays. He called to Helen to join him in the pool. Edgar took both the trays and set them down. He grabbed Helen's wrist. "C'mon, let's get wet."

Helen protested good-naturedly, saying she certainly wasn't going to jump into the pool wearing a dress, but Edgar was still feeling frisky. He wanted to do something impetuous. And he wanted to do it with Helen in front of their family and friends. He wanted them all to see how she made him feel.

Despite her resistance, he pulled her toward the pool. His mood was so elevated that he did not notice that the tone of her protestations had changed from playful to serious. He moved so fast in his elation that he did not hear the genuine fear that had crept into her voice. The hysteria. He had made up his mind; he was taking her in.

Helen raked her nails down Edgar's arm. Drawing blood. "I

said no!" she screamed in a shrill voice that echoed in the back-yard. All eyes were on the two of them. The only sound was the lapping of pool water. Nobody knew what to say, and they felt that it was up to Edgar or Helen to break the spell.

The side gate of the fence opened and Martha walked through.

"Nobody answered the front door, so I figured—"

She looked at the solemn faces, took in the silent atmosphere, and said, "You call this a party? Jesus, you could at least turn on the radio."

That broke the spell. Attention was diverted. Folks started moving again.

Helen told Edgar in a low, apologetic voice, "I don't . . . I don't swim. When I was little—"

Edgar put his finger to her lips. "It was my fault. I'm so sorry."

"Me too."

Helen grabbed Martha and introduced her around as an old friend. Steve offered her a beer and Martha declined. "No thank you, dear. I would rip this joint up."

As they all settled into quiet conversations about nothing much at all, Kelly said to her boss, "On your finger. Is that what I think it is?" and pointed to the solitaire diamond-and-gold band on Helen's left ring finger. Helen held her hand out for everybody to see. "Yesterday. At the justice of the peace." Through the oohs and ahhs, a shadow crossed Jane's face. She looked at Edgar and said, "I'm so happy for you, Edgar. I'm so happy for both of you."

Jane hugged the newlyweds, but it was stilted and stiff.

And anytime Edgar happened to glance at Martha, he found that she would avert her eyes.

Martha and Helen retreated to the kitchen. Elmore manned the grill while the rest of the adults sat around the pool. Tyler and Savannah were wearing water wings and splashing around in the shallow end. Edgar waded in with them just to be extra safe.

Edgar held Savannah while she kicked at the water, drops exploding like rhinestones in the summer sun. The air needed to be cleared with Jane. She was hurting for her sister. Edgar wanted to do it now while Helen was in the house.

"I'm sorry if all of this is bizarre. It wasn't something I just rushed into. I hate to say I've moved on, because I'll never move on. Never."

"No, Edgar. I like Helen. I really do. I truly am happy to see you build a life."

"But . . ."

"But nothing. I like Helen. And I'm happy for you."

Steve said, "Edgar, she's great."

They sat for a while and watched Edgar play with the children in the pool. The air hadn't quite been cleared yet, and they all knew it. Something remained unspoken.

Jane said, "Helen really is great. I like her. If I seem off, it's just that maybe I like her too goddamn much. Maybe I feel guilty for liking Helen. Judy was my sister . . . And it's hard for me to see you move past her."

"I told you. I never will."

"I know. I know that. It was time anyway. I know that. It was time. It's just hard."

The July sun glinted off Edgar's glasses, hiding his eyes. "It was time to let go and let God."

"That's AA-speak," Steve said.

"And God forgive me for asking this, but I have to know—"

"Yes," Edgar said. "It's Judy's ring."

"Why on earth would you do that? It's ghoulish. If you need the money for a new ring, we'll—"

"I wanted Judy to be a part of this. An equal part. Like a triangle. All sides equal. No one side more or less than the other two."

Jane nodded and pulled Savannah out of the pool and began to dry her off with a towel.

Edgar went inside for dry clothes. He walked down the hallway, a towel draped around his shoulders, but stopped outside the guest bathroom. He heard a hushed, urgent voice coming from inside. It was Martha's voice.

In general, Edgar was not one to eavesdrop. And he certainly had never done so outside a bathroom, but there was something about Martha that hit him wrong. The way he would catch her looking at him and then look away. He was beginning to wonder if she was a lesbian with a crush on Helen. Or maybe he was just imagining things because he was a little jealous of the bond they shared. But her voice grew more heated and he quite clearly heard her say, "Just break his fucking fingers," and then something that sounded like, "Give him a Post-it note," and then something about working with gamblers.

The bathroom door swung open without prelude—Martha in midsentence on her cell phone. She stared at Edgar and ended the call without notice to the other party. Martha reached back into the bathroom and grabbed a can of deodorizing spray. She handed it to Edgar.

"Sorry, dear."

In their bedroom, Helen held her arms crossed in front of her.

"I just don't like her," Edgar said. "She was talking violence. She said something about breaking somebody's fingers."

"That's just . . . she's a good person. You were listening outside the bathroom? Jesus."

"She's a crafty-eyed bitch."

"A crafty-eyed what? Are you kidding me? What does that even mean?"

"You know what it means."

"I most certainly do not. This is a whole new facet of your personality. A scary facet."

"I just want to protect what's mine."

"What's yours? Am I an object now? A puzzle box you can display in your glass case?"

"She's a criminal. That stuff about conning the waitress? Think about it. Stalking people? Photographing them? Breaking their fingers?"

"Everything except spying on people while they're using the bathroom. Maybe we should get one of those nanny cams for over the toilet."

"I don't like her, okay? I don't trust her."

"Okay. But I do. I trust her with everything."

"Fine."

"Fine. Jesus, Edgar. What's wrong with us? We've been married one day and we've had our first and second fight. Plus a little spousal battery thrown in."

Edgar thought it over. "Well, you didn't drink. And I didn't feel guilty. Win-win."

"Let's see if we can wrap this thing up without a knife fight."

"I was thinking more along the lines of a duel."

Helen uncovered a plate of deviled eggs that Martha had brought.

"I have a platter for these somewhere. I saw it the other day."

Martha watched Helen rummage through the undercounter cabinet.

"You make amends wherever possible. Wherever possible. It's simply not possible to bring this man's wife back. Nor his unborn child. What you're doing is . . . something else entirely."

Helen stacked pots and containers on the floor as she went through the cabinet. She pulled out a dusty bottle of brandy. It was labeled *Edgar and Judy* and decorated with a drawing of a bride and groom. A commemorative from their wedding.

Martha and Helen exchanged a look.

"Oh dear, that just has to be an omen."

Helen replaced the bottle and pulled out the egg platter.

"He lost a wife and he lost a child. Because of me. Because I'm an alcoholic. But I've corrected it. Now I'm his wife. And I can give him a child. I can make amends."

"Maybe it will work out for you."

Helen looked Martha in the eyes and said, "Edgar doesn't like you."

"What?"

"Edgar doesn't like you."

"Oh, well then, that's that."

"He thinks you're a criminal."

"Oh. That business about breaking fingers. He heard. Well, he heard wrong. It's a joke. I'm tracking down a man for one of my clients. A man with gambling debts. The joke is that instead of breaking his fingers like some loan shark, I leave him Post-it notes. At his work. His church. His home. To embarrass him. It's silly."

"You are a criminal."

"No, I used to be a criminal. And when you get right down to it, we're all criminals, aren't we? Ms. Cover-Up."

"I think I want a new sponsor. I think I don't want a sponsor at all. I'm done with the program."

"Dear—"

"That part of my life is over. No hard feelings. But it's over."

"Helen—"

55555

Grant Jerkins

"It's over. I don't want to hear it. I have to do what makes Edgar happy. That's my program."

"Whatever you like. I won't argue. Just promise me one thing. If you feel like you're going to pick up a drink, call me before you do it."

152

39

IF YOU KNEW WHAT
YOU WERE LOOKING FOR

Helen parked her car at the far end of the Walgreens parking lot. Neatly taped to the back window was a *For Sale* sign with her and Edgar's phone number. She'd told Edgar she wanted something new. They had already put her house on the market. Values were dismal right now, but she was upside down on her mortgage and needed to get out from under before it all came crashing down. So if she was selling her house, why not her car? A new start all the way around.

Inside, she browsed for a bit. She was wearing shorts and a halter top against the summer heat, but found it uncomfortably cool inside the store. At the makeup counter, she picked out some blush from an array of samples, tilted an oval mirror to reflect her face, and brushed some on. She found it too stark and wiped it off. She selected another and tried it. Too muted. She leaned across the counter to select a third sample. When she leaned away from the mirror, what Helen did not see was the reflection of the man who had been watching her since she came into the store. His image was perfectly reflected in the oval frame, like a portrait. The man had jet-black hair, greasy, and combed straight back. A pink scar marred his otherwise pale forehead, and his top lip drooped inward a bit because of the two front teeth he was missing—otherwise Mr. Slick-Back looked just as he did the night Helen gave him her last dance as a drunkard. Her last one-night stand.

When Helen leaned back into the mirror, the portrait of Mr. Slick-Back was replaced by her own image—as though Helen's life had been reduced to a series of images on a child's View-Master disk.

She never saw him.

The man took another step toward Helen. He leaned in and looked as though he were trying to catch the scent of her hair. Helen sensed the presence and turned around, but he was gone.

Helen grabbed her shopping buggy and started pushing it. She needed to get what she had come here for.

The man fell in behind her.

At the end of one of the aisles near the pharmacy was a discreet sign: *Family Planning Center*. This was where Helen stopped. There was a baffling array of home pregnancy test kits, and Helen began reading the backs of the boxes. Mr. Slick-Back sidled past her and looked over her shoulder to see exactly what Helen was shopping for. When she turned to him, he simultaneously turned to the opposite row of shelves and pretended that he had found exactly what he'd been looking for—KY Jelly, the warming kind.

Helen finally selected a kit that came with two units—a backup, she supposed, in case you peed on it wrong. She dropped it into her cart and headed for the front of the store.

One aisle over, the man matched her progress, step for step.

At the end of the aisle, Helen U-turned to head up the aisle Mr. Slick-Back had been coming down.

At the last possible second, the man pivoted on his heels and appeared to be simply strolling up the aisle by the time Helen and her cart completed the turn.

Helen followed just a step or two behind the man whose teeth marks were still just barely visible on her left breast, but only if you knew what you were looking for.

Mr. Slick-Back stopped and grabbed a package of Just For Men hair dye. Jet black. When Helen was past him, he shoved the box down the front of his pants.

Helen turned back to the family planning center. She returned the double test kit and selected the less expensive single version. *She was a licensed veterinarian, for Christ's sake. She could pee on a stick and get it right the first time.*

On her way to the front of the store, Helen picked up a few citronella candles from an endcap display because not only were they good to have on hand, but she really didn't want the pregnancy test kit to be the only object she placed on the checkout counter. She wanted to camouflage it somewhat. She stopped at the jewelry and fragrance counter and grabbed a pair of cheap opalescent earrings from a spin rack. They were big and gaudy. Perfect.

Three citronella candles, a pair of ugly earrings, and one home pregnancy test. The very definition of idle purchases.

She placed her items in front of the cashier, an elderly lady with a face like soft white leather. She rang up the candles first, then the earrings, and when she scanned the home pregnancy test kit, she smiled at Helen. The well-educated veterinarian blushed. Feeling awkward and self-conscious, Helen swiped her debit card through the terminal and keyed in her PIN. Replacing the card in her wallet, she knocked over a small display box of chewing gum. Helen and the customer behind her bent down at the same time to pick up the scattered packs of gum. Crouched on the floor, she met his eyes. Froze, as recognition set in. She remembered exactly who he was.

The man smiled, and his missing front teeth gave his face a vapid, evil quality.

Helen grabbed her purchases and ran.

The card receipt printed out, and the cashier tore it from the printer and held it out to Helen—who was disappearing through the door. "Guess she was embarrassed."

Mr. Slick-Back snatched the slip of paper from the woman's fingers. "I'll be most happy to reunite that young lady with her receipt."

The elderly cashier noted not only the pack of chewing gum that Mr. Slick-Back still held in his hand, but also the top of the hair dye box peeking over the waist of his pants. "Sir, you have to pay—" But the man was gone.

The woman picked up the store telephone, punched the intercom button, and calmly spoke the code words that would alert security to the crime of shoplifting.

In the parking lot, Mr. Slick-Back was in time to see Helen slam her car door. As the car backed out of the parking space, the man began to repeat something to himself. Over and over he repeated the numbers. The phone number on the *For Sale* sign in the back window of Helen's car.

The white-haired cashier emerged from the store, a stout security man in tow, and pointed a finger of accusation at Mr. Slick-Back.

Mr. Slick-Back turned around, Helen's receipt in one hand, the pack of gum in the other, and the top of the Just For Men package poking out of his pants.

"God damn," he said.

40

GOLD TEETH AND PLATINUM GRILLS GLINTING IN THE SUN

The judge peered down from his nest-like perch at the forlorn Cornell Smith—aka Mr. Slick-Back. The judge motioned for the evidence bag lying on the prosecution's table. The bailiff retrieved it and handed it to the judge.

His Honor removed the pack of gum and the box of hair dye from the plastic bag and considered both of these items.

"Third offense. One hundred twenty days."

The judge tossed the pack of gum down from his bench. Cornell caught it neatly.

"Enjoy your gum."

"God damn," said Cornell.

"Fine. Make it a hundred and fifty."

Mr. Smith started mumbling something under his breath,

and the judge was about to up the ante yet again, when he realized Cornell was only reciting a string of numbers. Sounded like a phone number. The judge let it pass.

He'd been in jail before, but the most he'd ever done was thirty days in city lockup. Now he had to do five times that.

Cornell made his way down a concrete-and-steel corridor carrying his jail-issue belongings and thought about how he came to be here. He'd been surprised she'd remembered him. He didn't think she would. He had thought a lot about her since the accident. Wondered on more than one occasion what might have happened between them. Cornell had been looking to connect with someone. They'd both been pretty drunk. He'd figured he'd look just like anybody else to her. He'd not been in a blackout that night, but he was pretty sure she had been. Cornell understood blackouts. But she'd remembered, all right. And she'd been scared. Scared. Wonder why?

A guard opened the cell door, and Cornell stepped inside his new home—which was already occupied. To himself, Cornell said *God damn* as he looked over his cellmate: a three-hundred-pounder, stubbly head with rings of fat circling his massive neck. And covered in tattoos. Aryan. *Yep, God damn.* The man's eyes had a vacant look that reminded Cornell of the way his mentally retarded nephew never seemed to really focus his gaze. And there was a lethal, casual evil lurking in those eyes as well.

Though he had done two weeks here and thirty days there, Cornell had always done those stretches in the pissant city jail.

This was county. A whole different ball game. He was working his way up. Cornell grinned (conscious of exposing his missing front teeth) and said, "Very happy to be sharing my cell with a regular white man, I can tell you that much."

The cellmate took Cornell's blanket and towel away from him and placed them on his own bed. The man turned back around, smiled, and poked his grimy stub of a finger into Cornell's mouth, probing the gummy gap.

"Smooth," the man said.

God damn. God damn. God damn.

In the community room, Cornell played Mario Brothers on the wall-mounted television. He was *killing*. He moved his whole body with each move of the joystick. Six or seven other inmates stood around them, admiring Cornell's proficiency.

The observers parted when Cornell's cellmate approached. The massive Aryan snatched the game controller away from Cornell and said, "Game over, droop lip." On the screen, Luigi fell over a cliff, screaming, *"Mama mia!"*

Now Cornell had seen *Oz* on his stolen HBO, and he knew that this situation would mark him either as everybody's target or as a fighter not to be messed with.

"Now, now. If you want to play, you only need but ask. No need for personal insults. For instance, I would never dream of mentioning the urine stain on the front of your pants. A toileting accident of some kind, I would imagine."

The Aryan shifted his belly to afford himself a view of his

own crotch. At that moment, Cornell rocketed upward and grabbed hold of the joystick. He shoved with every bit of strength that he had and rammed the joystick straight into the Aryan's mouth. A vicious knee straight into the giant's crotch brought him to his knees. From that position, Cornell began to hammer the joystick into the man's mouth, the force of the blows taking the Aryan the rest of the way to the floor. Cornell kept hammering, and he thought he felt a tooth break. Maybe two.

He kept pounding, skull-fucking the son of a bitch with the joystick. The other inmates whooped and hollered. When he heard someone say, "Guard," Cornell climbed off and joined the circle of onlookers.

As his days wore on, Cornell enjoyed the freedom that his one act of bravado had purchased him. He could move around freely—within reason.

He sat by himself in the dirt of the exercise yard and watched a group of black inmates lifting weights. He sat at the outskirts of what they would have considered their space. What drew him to them was that quite a few of these men were missing teeth, and, unlike Cornell, their missing teeth had been replaced with gold, silver, and platinum ones.

Cornell had read one book during the thirty-five years of his life. That book was *The Great Gatsby*. He had been in a state-run boys' home at the time, and all the older kids had been assigned that book to read for English class. Cornell saw the book everywhere. Not having a copy made him feel left out. So he stole one.

And he read it. He read it proudly, out in the open, so he could be observed in the reading of it (except by the original owner). He had started by just pretending to read it, to belong to the group he considered somehow elite, but the damnedest thing happened. He didn't so much fall in love with the book as he fell in love with Jay Gatsby. Jay Gatsby was the shit. Jay Gatsby had started with nothing, just a poor kid in love with some girl. Jay Gatsby became rich. He broke a few rules along the way, a few shady deals, but he did it. He didn't really get the girl in the end, but still he made out all right. Besides, the girl, Daisy, was a stone-cold killer. Gatsby was all right. And more than anything else, he liked the way Gatsby talked. It was all *old sport* this and *old sport* that, but if you replaced *old sport* with *fuckwad*—it made perfect sense. Yep, Gatsby was the shit. And that was how Cornell saw himself. Just still stuck in poor mode. And, Cornell was certain, should Jay Gatsby lose a tooth or two, he'd replace them with gold.

For some, such an anecdote might be the preamble to a life-long love affair with literature, but this was not the case with Cornell. No, one book was plenty, thank you.

And so Cornell Smith sat in the dirt and watched the black inmates build their muscles, their gold teeth and platinum grills glinting in the sun.

He picked up a twig and scratched the numbers in the dirt.

Cornell gathered his few belongings. A guard waited for him just outside the open cell door. The days had been slow to pass, but they had passed.

Carrying his things out the door, Cornell stopped and went back to his cellmate, stretched out on the bottom bunk.

Cornell inserted his finger into the Aryan's mouth, probing the toothless opening.

"Smooth. Old sport."

Cornell signed the release form, and the female correctional officer pushed a manila envelope under the chain-link screen. He opened the envelope and withdrew his wallet and keys. His fingers dug around the bottom and scooped out a crumpled scrap of paper. It was Mrs. Woolrich's Walgreens receipt. Yes, he knew her name. He knew where she lived. Inmates weren't allowed Internet access, but one guy had a contraband Black-Berry. Cornell had paid him twenty dollars to do a reverse lookup of the memorized phone number. In less than fifteen seconds, he had the name Edgar Woolrich and a Mantissa Cove address. There was something about that name. Cornell could swear he knew an Edgar Woolrich, but he couldn't place him. It was a memory that was just out of reach, tantalizing him.

Lastly, Cornell found the pack of chewing gum in the envelope. He unwrapped it and inserted a flat rectangular piece into his slack mouth.

The trailer was paid for free and clear, and the lot was paid for up front every six months, so paying the rent hadn't been an issue.

Cornell was greeted by stale musty air when he entered his double-wide, carrying a twelve-pack of Natural Light—the post-incarceration beer of choice.

The electricity was flowing thanks to a four-hundred-yard length of power cable patched in to his closest neighbor's transformer. He lit a cigarette, flipped on the television (a satellite hack he'd purchased at a pawnshop), and settled down on the couch. An old movie from the seventies was playing. He'd seen it before. Jodie Foster was just a kid in this one. She had killed her parents or something like that and was living the life. Except Martin Sheen was snooping around. Wouldn't leave her alone. He was some kind of child molester or something. This was the part where she was giving old Martin some cyanide-laced tea. Tastes of almonds, he said. That's just the almond cookies, young Jodie reassured him.

Cornell studied the drugstore receipt. He added to it the piece of paper on which he had written Edgar Woolrich's name, address, and phone number. That name. It still bothered him. He got up and went to the bathroom. In the cabinet under the sink, Cornell found the newspaper he had been holding on to for well over a year. He hadn't studied it or obsessed over it. He did not return to it from time to time to contemplate or explore shades of guilt and culpability. But he *had* saved it. Yes, he had saved it. He opened the paper to the article about the fatal hit-and-run accident. It featured a photograph of Edgar and Judy Woolrich. The photo had come from a Teacher of the Year award ceremony.

Edgar and Judy Woolrich. What the fuck was going on here?

Cornell looked at himself in the toothpaste-spattered mirror. The scar on his forehead was pink and stood out in contrast with his pale skin. He touched it, remembering. Drunken laughter. Loud music. Groping hands. Their car drifting into the oncoming lane. The laughter cut short as white light welled up in the car. Picking glass out of his bleeding forehead. Turning and spitting his teeth into the backseat in a stream of blood and thick saliva. And seeing the other car, overturned and lying in the ditch. And mumbled words.

We've got to go.

What?

Now!

What happened?

We've got to go. Now!

The images and the words faded from his mind, and Cornell was left with only his own image reflected in the mirror. He grinned. He suspected there was opportunity here, although he still did not understand what exactly had transpired.

He noticed that his hair had grown out considerably. The dirty-blond roots clashed with the deep black. Especially at the widow's peak. From the cabinet drawer he took a black Magic Marker and began the chore of touching up his roots.

From a gas station, Cornell called the phone number. A man, presumably Edgar Woolrich, answered. Cornell inquired about the car for sale.

"The car was sold several months ago."

"Oh. A friend of mine talked to the lady. Judy Woolrich?"

There was a long pause. Then: "No. Helen. Helen Woolrich. It's sold. Good-bye."

He parked a safe distance away. Using the binoculars he'd five-finger-discounted at Goodwill, Cornell watched Edgar Woolrich string Christmas lights along the eaves of his house. The woman he'd followed at Walgreens (Helen Woolrich?) held the ladder for him. Her lower abdomen was heavy and swollen.

Cornell held up the newspaper photo and compared. The man was clearly Edgar Woolrich. No doubt about it. Helen, his Helen, had replaced the deceased Judy Woolrich.

What the fuck, old sport?

Cornell grinned, exposing his toothless gap.

What the fuck indeed.

41

IT'S A WONDERFUL LIFE

She was still somewhat disconcerted by the sudden emergence of her belly. She hadn't shown at all for most of the first five months, and now coming into her sixth month, seemingly overnight, she was sporting a good size belly.

As she reached down to retrieve the Saturday mail that had fallen through the front door slot, Helen lost sight of it because of her protruding stomach and scooped it up blindly.

She tossed the mail onto the foyer table without looking at it. Edgar was the bill payer, and so she did not see that one of the mail pieces was addressed to Helen Woolrich in thick block letters.

Helen returned to the living room, where she had been hanging glass ornaments on the Christmas tree.

Mitzi watched Edgar squint through his bifocals as he methodically examined a string of old-fashioned blue cluster lights that he could not get to light. He visually inspected and reset each bulb, plugging and unplugging the strand, but with no success. He finally saw that one of the clusters was missing a tiny bulb.

"Found it. Missing bulb. These are wired to not light if there's a bulb missing. Safety feature. We don't have anything to replace it with."

"Maybe you should just throw them out. Get the new LED kind."

Edgar fingered the empty socket, frowning.

"Edgar. Really. Just throw them out."

There was a time that Edgar would not have been able to let something like that go. A time when he would have combed the house for that missing bulb. Instead, he took the string of lights to the kitchen and shoved them into the trash can.

When he came back, Helen handed him the tinsel-encrusted angel, and Edgar placed it perfectly atop the tree.

Later, while Helen was snuggled up under an afghan, an empty bag of microwave popcorn on the floor beside her, watching *It's a Wonderful Life*, Edgar grabbed the mail and sat down on the couch between Helen and Mitzi. He rubbed Mitzi behind her ears in the spot she liked best. He liked the dog just fine, but the cats had been a big adjustment for him. Agnes, a sinewy yellow tabby (that Helen said was actually called an orange tabby, or red if you wanted to be technical), generally kept her distance. But the other one, Molly, a striking black-and-white with spooky green eyes, had taken a shine to him. Whenever Edgar sat down or in any way created a horizontal plane with his body, Molly positioned herself there, purring and rubbing. Sometimes, in the dead of night, Edgar would awaken to find the cat butting his forehead with hers. Edgar held the mail higher above his lap than he would have normally liked—to make sure Molly had room to curl up there. It was an adjustment. As were the litter boxes.

Normally, going through the mail was a chore reserved for his desk, but Edgar wanted to be on the couch with Helen near the tree and the animals. He carefully slit open each envelope. He did this to the one addressed to Helen. He was in the act of prying it open and extracting its contents when he saw that it was addressed to her.

He tossed it to her.

Helen sat up a little, not wanting to come too far out from under the afghan. She opened the envelope and extracted a small piece of paper. It was a Walgreens sales receipt. For three citronella candles, a pair of earrings, and one home pregnancy test kit. The receipt was dated over five months ago. She knew immediately what it was and who had sent it.

She turned the receipt over and saw on the back, penciled in block letters: *DOES HE KNOW YOU KILLED HIS WIFE?*

Helen's body stiffened and her mind went gray.

"What is it?"

Helen was unable to respond.

"Helen?"

She broke her eyes away from the words, pulled her mind

from the opaque grayness that had swallowed it. She couldn't quite find her voice, so she looked at Edgar and raised her eyebrows.

"What is it?"

"Oh. It's uh—it's an old bill."

Edgar reached for it.

Helen pulled back.

"Give it to me. I'll pay it."

"No. I mean it—it's actually a receipt, see?"

She held the face of it out for Edgar to see, in the spot where she knew neither prism of his bifocals could focus very well. Edgar squinted and nodded.

"I must have left it at the store and they mailed it to me."

"That's odd."

Helen placed the receipt back in the envelope and tossed it on the coffee table as though it meant absolutely nothing to her.

"I guess some people are just very thorough."

"I can relate," Edgar said, grinning. He rubbed her pregnant stomach. "Want some more popcorn?"

"You know what? I do."

Edgar grabbed the empty bag off the floor and headed into the kitchen to make more popcorn.

Helen stared at the envelope, afraid to move, afraid to take her eyes off it, as though it were a king cobra poised to strike.

From the kitchen, Edgar called out, "But I wonder how they got your address? Odd."

"Yeah, that is odd. It's from when I bought the pregnancy test." *Why did she say that? That just made it seem even weirder.*

Helen heard the electronic beeps of microwave buttons being pressed. She slowly reached her arm out toward the envelope, never taking her eyes off it, like an Indian snake charmer. She heard Edgar returning from the kitchen and jerked her hand back.

Edgar cleared all the mail from the coffee table—leaving Helen's envelope. He made it halfway to his desk before turning on his heels.

"If it has to do with the baby, that's medical, potentially deductible."

He scooped up the envelope.

Helen grimaced. "You're so thorough."

"That's me."

Edgar took it to his desk in the nook just outside the foyer. The charts and graphs had been removed from the walls around his work area and carefully filed away, but Edgar's desk remained obscenely neat and ordered.

Edgar sat down at the desk, counted to three, and there was Molly in his lap. He booted up the computer and began to methodically separate the mail, tossing the advertising circulars in the wastebasket.

From the kitchen, the microwave chirped to signal that it had completed its task.

"Edgar . . ."

Edgar smiled and got up.

Helen peered over the back of the couch. She could see the envelope in the stack. It was grimy and off-white compared to the others. She contemplated whether there would be enough time to dash over to the desk and grab the receipt. How would she look if caught in the act? She decided not to risk it and squeezed Edgar's hand warmly when he brought her the bag of popcorn.

Edgar logged into their checking account and issued a payment for the gas bill. Helen watched him. Her envelope was next in line to be paid or filed. Edgar picked it up and opened it. The receipt was in his hands. Helen could see the hateful words printed on the back. She could actually feel the twitch in Edgar's wrist as he began to reflexively turn it over.

Helen cried out in anguish.

Edgar was on his feet instantaneously.

"What?"

"It's the baby. It hurts."

Edgar was kneeling beside her, rubbing her convex middle.

"No, not there. It's my back. I think she kicked my kidney. Go to the bedroom and get me the heating pad."

As soon as Edgar cleared the stairs, Helen was on her feet. She snatched the envelope and receipt off the desk.

She headed for the kitchen with it, changed her mind and dashed into the living room, Mitzi galloping behind her, excited by her owner's excitement.

Helen tucked the envelope and receipt under the couch. She changed her mind again, scooped it up, and ran to the kitchen trash can. She shoved the damning note deep into the trash, ran back into the living room, and leaped onto the sofa seconds before Edgar returned with the heating pad.

The Ninth Step

What the hell was she thinking? He would notice the receipt was gone. He would ask her what had happened to it. He wouldn't let it go.

Edgar tucked the heating pad under Helen and plugged it in.

"I want ice cream."

"I'll fix you a bowl. Just give me a second."

"Is it butter pecan?"

"No."

"I need butter pecan."

Edgar sighed and Helen gave him her best puppydog eyes.

He put on his coat and picked up the car keys.

"You realize it's ten degrees outside?"

"The baby wants ice cream. Butter pecan."

Edgar sighed again and looked down at his feet. Something on the carpet glinted and caught his eye. He bent over to retrieve it.

"Hey, look, here's that bulb."

He held it close to his face and gave the bulb the old Edgar Woolrich once-over.

"I bet I can get that strand to work."

He went into the kitchen, and Helen followed him.

"Can't that wait till later? The baby needs ice cream."

Edgar yanked the tangled string of lights from the trash can. Several pieces of trash fell out as he pulled on the strand.

Including the receipt.

Note side up.

In horror, Helen watched from the doorway.

175

"Honey, please? Now? Please?"

Edgar grumbled and scooped all of the trash back into the can. He kissed Helen's forehead on his way out.

Helen retrieved the note and tucked it into her bra.

The earrings. She would tell him that she needed the receipt to return some earrings she'd bought that day.

But Edgar never asked. And nothing more came of it. Until two months later.

42

WE CAN HELP EACH OTHER

"So you've never been here before and you don't have an appointment?"

"That's right."

"And you don't have a pet?"

"You just tell Mrs. Woolrich that her driving partner's here."

From the treatment room passageway, Helen saw Kelly talking to her blackmailer and went with dread to speak to him.

Cornell smiled at Helen as though they were high school sweethearts reunited.

"Hey, Doc. How 'bout that ride you promised me?"

Very much conscious of Kelly observing this exchange, Helen said, "I don't think I have time right now, Mr. . . . ?"

"Oh, let's not do names."

"Well, I really don't have the time right now. Maybe later."

"Didn't imagine you would." Cornell held up a sealed envelope. "I was just hoping I could get this to the post office. Maybe you could . . ."

Helen took the grimy envelope.

Cornell tipped an imaginary hat to both Helen and Kelly. "Ladies."

Cornell turned to leave, then turned back and added, "You sure are pretty." And left.

Kelly turned to Helen and said, "Explanation."

"I'm doing volunteer work with the homeless."

"Names? Let's not do?"

Helen shrugged.

"That envelope. No address."

Helen realized that the envelope had no address or other markings—much less a stamp.

"The homeless are often also chronically mentally ill," she explained, as though to a child.

Helen went to her office and tore open the envelope. On a scrap of paper inside was written: *$10,000.00.*

Helen wanted a drink. She very much wanted just one drink.

In the pawnshop, Helen filled out a pawn ticket. She signed her name, pulled the wedding ring that had once belonged to Judy Woolrich from her finger, and slid it under the chain-link barrier behind which a bearded and tattooed man stood. The pawnbroker counted out a mound of hundred-dollar bills. He pushed the stack of cash under the barrier to Helen.

* * *

That night, Edgar held Helen's naked hand and told her not to cry, that everything was going to be all right.

He picked up the phone and said to Helen, "Thank God I thought to have it laser etched."

Helen's stomach knotted, and she wondered to herself how all this stress would affect the baby.

"Yes. Thank God. You're so thorough."

Edgar spoke into the phone, "Yes, I'd like to report a theft."

It was a warm day for February, with bright sunshine. At an isolated rest stop beyond the city, Helen and Cornell sat at a weathered concrete table. Helen nudged an envelope across the pitted cement surface toward Cornell.

Cornell ripped it open greedily. He frowned.

"Well now, that's a long way shy of ten grand."

He reached across the table and took hold of Helen's wrist.

"I was gonna get my teeth fixed."

Helen jerked free of his grasp and said, "I can't help you. I have no way to get money."

"Sure you do."

"You don't understand. His life is numbers. If I take money out of our accounts, he'll know."

"That sounds like a *you* problem, not a *me* problem. Sell something."

"I don't have anything left to sell."

"Oh, I don't know about that. You got that brand-new SUV you drove up in. And that house you live in."

"It's not mine. I can't just—"

"You're married, right? Then it's half yours." Cornell smiled, struck by an insight. "And what's half yours is half mine. Now that's just good math."

"If the point of me paying you off is to keep Edgar from finding out, then selling our house will more or less tip him off that something is very wrong."

"Again, your problem."

"This is insane."

Helen got up and walked toward the parking area. If she hadn't been so pregnant, she would have run. Cornell caught up to her and roughly grabbed her by the upper arm, turning her around. Helen jerked away, grunting with pain. They both stared at the angry red fingerprints now forming just below her biceps.

Cornell looked more hurt than Helen.

"I never—I never meant . . ."

"Well, you did. Why don't you leave me alone?"

Helen was crying now. Partly because the pregnancy hormones left her emotions raw, and partly because she saw that Cornell was feeding into it. He looked greatly disturbed.

"I just figured you had money, that's all. I like you. I thought you might like me too. Want to help me. That's all."

"Like you? You're ruining my life."

"We can help each other. You help me get money, I'll help you . . . Keep your life from messing up. It don't have to be ugly."

43

NICE GUN

Detective Poole and her partner were waiting at the counter when Edgar walked into the pawnshop. Poole was looking at a .357 Smith & Wesson inside a glass case.

"Nice gun," Edgar said.

"You a gun buff?"

"Hardly. Never owned one. Never plan to."

"Good. I don't advocate gun ownership by private citizens."

"Is this why—"

"Look, Mr. Woolrich, this isn't my beat, you know that." Poole seemed to be speaking more to the gun than to Edgar. "But the way I see it, we've got history. I know things have been bad for you. And to be honest, I haven't missed our weekly meetings. I was glad to get you out of my life. I was glad you moved on."

Poole now looked Edgar in the eyes.

"But sometimes, people make bad decisions."

Poole nodded to the pawnbroker, and he handed her a ring. Poole handed it to Edgar.

"You found it."

"Yep."

Poole nodded again to the pawnbroker. He reached his serpentine tattooed arms above his head to the closed-circuit monitor mounted on the wall. He swiveled it so that the screen was facing Edgar. The digital footage was already cued up, so the man just hit the "play" button on the security console.

The monitor showed a blocky, flickering video image of a woman pulling the ring off her finger. As the woman leaned forward to push the ring across the counter, her face filled the screen. The pawnbroker paused the video. There could be no mistake. It was Helen.

Detective Poole watched Edgar's face undergo a series of changes. It was like watching a mime enact the five Kübler-Ross stages of death and dying: denial and anger, then bargaining and depression, finally settling on acceptance.

Edgar stared at Helen's frozen image on the screen. And when he spoke, he spoke to that image.

"Yes, sometimes people do make bad decisions."

Edgar turned to Detective Poole.

"Do they sometimes get a second chance?"

Poole nodded.

44

WHAT IT WOULD BE LIKE
HAVING YOUR BABY BORN IN JAIL

Helen grabbed the thick sheaf of bills from the ATM and made her way back to the car. She plopped behind the steering wheel, her belly pulling her down. She handed the wad of cash over to Cornell, who was busy rummaging through her purse. He stopped long enough to count the bills.

"That's the daily limit," Helen said.

"Like I said, I'm not out to hurt you, but you got a lot of thinking to do. About how bad you wanna keep that new husband of yours. Or what it would be like having your baby born in jail."

Cornell got out of the car. Helen watched in the rearview mirror as he disappeared into the night. And farther off in the distance, the beckoning warm neon glow of a liquor store.

She looked down at her hands. They were shaking.

Helen knew that if it were not for the baby growing inside her, she would drink. She would drink and drink and drink until it killed this feeling. So she could escape it, even if just for one night, she could escape it. *What had she done? What had she brought on herself and Edgar?*

She looked down at her hands again. They were shaking even worse than before.

45

JUST ANOTHER LIE

Edgar came home to find the house empty and dark. The cats were mewing their hunger, and Mitzi was scratching at the back door.

Edgar checked his cell phone. There had been no missed calls. He checked the landline. No messages. Helen had not tried to contact him, and her cell phone had been turned off.

He looked up a number in the phone book and dialed it.

"Yes, I'm looking for meetings in the Mantissa Cove area."

Edgar felt self-conscious walking into the church basement. The meeting was already in progress. Helen had more or less stopped going to meetings after her break-off with Martha.

An overweight, balding businessman was standing and speaking to the group.

". . . So I came to believe that a power greater than myself could restore me to sanity . . ."

If Helen had been at this meeting, she would have recognized this man as the adulterer she and Martha had followed to a hotel and photographed.

". . . I knew that even though I was powerless over alcohol, God is not. God is stronger."

Edgar scanned the group and saw Martha in a green nylon tracksuit, sipping coffee from a lipstick-stained foam cup.

". . . I guess I finally understood that stupid bumper sticker on my sponsor's car. I let go and let God."

In the church parking lot, people stood in small groups to talk and smoke cigarettes.

Edgar stood with Martha next to her old Malibu.

"That would be completely and wholly inappropriate. I couldn't possibly even think of speaking to you in regard to Helen."

For some reason, when he looked into her eyes, Edgar felt that just the opposite was true. Her eyes seemed to be saying that she actually wanted to tell Edgar something, but something— *was it honor?*—was holding her back.

"I understand, but that's not good enough. Something is wrong. Why would she sell her wedding ring? And then lie about it. We're not rich, but we've certainly got enough that we don't need to pawn our belongings for cash. She's hiding something."

"So you came to me?"

Again, her tone was one of derision, but her eyes seemed to say, *Of course you came to me, because I do know.*

"Tell me who I married."

"You married an alcoholic. Live with it."

"I have been. And now I need help. Helen needs help."

"If Helen's gotten herself into some kind of trouble, then that's between you and her. And God."

"You think she's in trouble?"

"I really wouldn't know."

Edgar felt certain that if he could just find the right word combination, Martha would open up.

"Of course you would. You're a con woman. A criminal."

"I never tried to hide who I am. Or who I used to be."

"Are you saying that Helen is trying to hide who she used to be?"

"I'm not saying anything. But I will say this: Sometimes it seems like we spend the second half of our lives trying to hide who we were during the first half. And that's doubly true for an alcoholic. *Comprende?*"

Frustrated, Edgar slapped his palm against the hood of Martha's car. It wasn't a particularly hard blow, but when he drew his hand away, the edge of his wedding band scraped the paint, leaving an ugly scratch.

"I'll be sending you a bill for that. This is a classic 1979 Malibu. And I just had it painted."

Embarrassed, Edgar trailed his finger along the damaged area. The paint job was old, pitted, and flaky. That was why it had scratched so easily.

"Just another lie," Edgar mumbled.

"Speak up, dear."

"What have you gotten her involved in? Why is she . . . Have you gotten her involved in something illegal?"

"Illegal? Helen? Please. I'm no angel. But Helen is."

Martha got in her car and started it. Before closing the door, she said, "And be on the lookout for the bill for the paint job."

46

HELEN = MURDER

Edgar paced between the kitchen and the living room. And Mitzi followed him back and forth. Molly watched from a shadowy corner, waiting for him to sit down so she could nestle in his lap.

He held Helen's wedding ring, stopping sometimes to inspect it, consider it, study it like a math problem. Circles, he remembered, were the pursuit of madmen.

He replayed the conversation with Martha over and over in his mind. She had seemingly told him nothing, but her eyes had sparked, tantalizing him.

We spend the second half of our lives trying to hide who we were during the first half.

And be on the lookout for the bill for the paint job.

Edgar went to the coat closet in the foyer and pulled out his long-unused tablet of wall chart paper. He tore out a blank page and spread it out over his desk, pushing the computer to the side to make room.

Edgar drew two columns, one labeled *Helen*, the other *Judy*.

HELEN	JUDY
On the road that night	*On the road that night*
Correct time frame	*Correct time frame*
Alcoholic	*Red paint on our car*
12 steps	*Dead 17 months*
Step 9—amends	
Black car	
Sober 17 months	

He drew lines matching up items from the two lists. He circled *BLACK CAR* and then opened his filing cabinet. He thumbed through the files, coming to one tabbed *Automobiles*. He pulled out title transfer papers from Helen's old car.

He opened an Internet browser window on the computer and Googled the term "VIN history." He tried a few of the results, but they weren't quite what he wanted. Then he selected a site called VIN Power that offered free vehicle identification number history searches.

Edgar entered the vehicle identification number from the title transfer paper. The results came up: 2005 Honda Insight.

It included body style, odometer reading, number of owners, engine size, and interestingly enough, exterior color. It was red.

Edgar crossed out *BLACK CAR* in Helen's column and replaced it with *RED*. He drew a connecting line from it to the entry *RED PAINT ON OUR CAR* under Judy's name.

Edgar dug back into his files and found printouts with automobile statistics along with his notebooks filled with car counts from his earlier research.

He tore out a clean sheet of chart paper and began the process:

Percent of cars on road at any given time that are red = 7%.

Type of red paint used by 3 auto makers—including Honda.

Paint type used on Honda.

Percent of cars on that road during time frame that are
*   Honda = 8%.*

Mean number of cars during time frame = 1377.

Percent of cars on road that are both red and Honda = 1.22%.

Percent of cars that meet all criteria = 0.75%.

Helen = repaired/repainted red Honda.

Edgar pulled out yet another of the bulging files of auto statistics that he had accumulated.

Although no repairs were listed in the report, Edgar felt that it was reasonable to assume that the car had been repainted during the course of repairs. But why to a different color? He hunted through the papers, scattering them. He found the figures he wanted and continued his list.

Percent chance of any car being repaired on any given day = 1.33%.

Percent chance of a red Honda being repaired on any given day = .06%.

Percent chance that repaired/repainted red car on road during time frame = .00013%.

Helen = repaired/repainted red Honda on road during time frame.

Percent chance that Helen's Honda was involved in the accident = 99.99987%.

Edgar looked over all of this information. He stared at the last line. Under it, he wrote:

Helen = Murder.

47

FISTS POISED TO STRIKE

It took her three tries to get the key into the front door.

She didn't see how she was going to be able to continue to hide this, but she was going to try. Any eventuality was better than seeing this dark knowledge reflected in Edgar's eyes.

The front door swung open into the dark house, leaving Helen silhouetted in the pale glow of the streetlight. She could make out Edgar sitting at his desk. If not for the dim light reflected off the familiar shape of his glasses, she would have thought that she'd walked in on an intruder.

"Why are you sitting in the dark? Are you okay?"

Edgar nodded.

"I had an emergency. I had to use cash. It was Kelly. She—"

Edgar stood up and held something out to Helen. She took it.

"You bought me a new ring? Oh Edgar." She flipped on the lights. "It's my ring. You found it? My ring. How?"

She looked up from the ring and saw the room. Papers strewn everywhere. Notebooks, bar graphs, statistics, printouts, formulas.

And then she saw the final equation.

HELEN = MURDER.

An animalistic grunt escaped from Edgar's tight lips; his eyes were sorrow and rage. And Helen had to look into those eyes and feel the despicable knowledge that they now shared.

Her worst nightmare had come true.

Unaware that she was even speaking, Helen began to chant almost inaudibly, "Oh Jesus, oh Jesus, oh Jesus, oh Jesus—"

The violent crack of Edgar's palm striking her face rang in the room like an accusation.

"Why?"

Edgar's hands squeezed into fists.

"Why?"

Helen scrambled backward, away from him. Her feet tangled in the thick paper folds of an overturned wall chart, and she fell to the floor.

Edgar towered over her, fists poised to strike.

"Do it."

He reared back.

"Do it."

This was what she wanted. Had wanted for so long. Punishment. Flagellation. Redemption. Her chance to finally be clean again.

But Edgar denied her. He was not yet capable. He lowered his fists.

Sobbing, Helen crawled away, struggled to her feet, and opened the sliding glass door to the backyard. Mitzi, who was watching the struggle from outside, nudged her owner. Helen pushed the dog away. She had only one objective. Punishment. She had to punish herself. She had to cauterize the flow of emotion that she could not bear to feel. If she had a gun, she would gladly put it to her temple and squeeze the trigger.

But there was no gun. There was the pool. And in its dark depths, she knew there would be redemption. True redemption.

Helen squeezed the trigger and jumped. The winter pool cover was in place. She landed squarely on the heavy-gauge plastic, jerking it loose from the side moorings. The thick tarp encased her descending body like a dry cocoon. And then the water penetrated, setting off chlorinated memories. She was hopelessly tangled now, submerged. She sank to the bottom of the pool where utter silence and final release awaited her.

She had been afraid. Afraid for so long. Afraid of the water. Afraid of Edgar finding out who she really was. And now he had. And now she embraced the water. And she had given Edgar what she knew he had always needed.

She opened her mouth and took the water deep into her lungs.

48

IT WAS ONLY FOR A MILLISECOND THAT HE PAUSED

He felt nothingness. There was no anger. No sorrow. No revelation. Only nothingness. Like Helen, he had sunk to the bottom of an abyss, but Edgar did not find release there.

He was vaguely aware of the dog barking in the backyard. That was a familiar sound and stood no chance of penetrating the abyss. But the barking had changed. There was an urgency to it. A differentness. It communicated emergency. It communicated that something was very wrong, and Edgar unwillingly climbed out from the nothingness to a conscious state.

He sat there, unable to move, his body not yet caught up with his mind. The barking grew ever more urgent, ever more insistent. He was finally able to break the inertia and ran for the back door.

Mitzi was perched at the edge of the pool, barking frantically at the water.

As he approached, Edgar saw bubbles coming up from the water. And Helen's murky, inert form floating face down, the thick plastic sheeting twisted around her.

Later, he would tell himself that it was only for a millisecond that he paused. That he dismissed the thought that flashed through his mind as soon as it made its unwelcome appearance. That he should do nothing. Let it be. Return to the house and call 911. Report an accidental drowning. Problem solved.

The baby. What about the baby?

But when Edgar later allowed himself to reflect on this dark moment, he knew that what had stopped him, or what had spurred him into action, was, yes, the baby she carried inside her, but also the knowledge that he could not allow himself to add to his already crushing burden of guilt.

He jumped into the pool.

He untangled her from the heavy tarp and dragged her body to the shallow end, heaving and pushing her up over the edge onto the cement decking. He straddled her, moaning and crying with rage and fear. He tilted her head back, pinched her nose shut, and blew air into her lungs.

It took only four rescue breaths before Helen's body responded. Her heart had never stopped beating. She was very much alive as her body convulsed and expelled the water she had taken in. She curled up on her side, racked with a coughing fit. Over and over. She vomited. Soon, she was gasping in watery, raspy breaths.

When she finally had a bit of strength, Helen crawled away like a wounded animal. She pulled herself under a patio table, curling her body around the base. And they both sat there, shivering in the night air, neither knowing what was next.

Thirty minutes had passed before Helen broke the silence. Her voice was a raspy, creaking wreck.

"I wanted to give back what I took."

Edgar was unable to respond, his face trembling with emotion. But he had to respond. It was time he unburdened himself. Not to her, not to Helen, but it was time to admit to himself why he had focused so much of his time and energy into finding the other driver. Why he needed someone else to be pronounced guilty.

"No."

"What?"

"No. You didn't kill her. I did. I wasn't watching the road. I was bidding on a puzzle box I wanted. I wasn't even looking at the road."

Later, out of their wet clothes and into warm pajamas, they sat at the kitchen table. Edgar made some decaffeinated coffee.

The wound had finally been lanced. Now it was time to probe and push, to get all the infection out. To be thorough.

"It was my fault. I've always known that. My fault. I could never admit it, but I've known it. So much easier to blame someone else. Or chaos. Randomness. I think some part of me felt that if I could track down the other driver, then I could stop blaming myself."

"I was drunk. Drunk out of my mind. When I saw my car the next morning. And the news. It was like I just turned into a robot—programmed with just one objective: Cover it up. And I did. I didn't think. I didn't feel. I just did."

Edgar nodded, listening.

"It was only later that I allowed myself to feel again. And when the emotions came, I couldn't live with them. I couldn't live with myself. I tried to kill myself. That didn't work. So I got sober. That worked. That worked."

"I can't even imagine you being drunk."

"Well, I was. But I still had to find a way to live with myself knowing the pain and suffering I'd caused."

"So you found me."

"So I found you. And I saw firsthand the damage I'd caused."

"You were drunk, yes. It could have just as easily been my fault."

"Even if it was you, if I hadn't been drunk I could have swerved—"

"I could have swerved."

"I'm just so sorry."

"Okay."

"Okay."

"So you found me. And you created this relationship with me."

"No. It's real, not created. I do love you. I love every neurotic bone in your body."

"I don't want to lose my wife and child. Not twice. I still want you. Us. Our baby. Our life."

Helen nodded, and the tears came again. She knew there was just one last bit of poison left in the wound. If they could clean it out, they might stand a chance.

Helen went and got the note. She'd never thrown it away. She handed it to Edgar.

"Somebody knows. He wants money."

49

THIS CRIME HAS TRANSFORMED HIM

During his free period, Edgar sat at his desk in the empty classroom.

The book, *Chaos and Crime*, sat unopened in front of him like a meal he was too full to eat, but knew he must.

He opened the book to the page he had marked. He had used the ugly little blackmail note as a place marker.

DOES HE KNOW YOU KILLED HIS WIFE?

Edgar read: *It takes but a small change in everyday factors to bring about victimization. The victim may desire to not be a victim. Remember, chaos cannot be predicted, but it can be controlled to an extent.*

Edgar looked up from the book to find Martin Kosinski standing in front of him.

204

The boy's nose was bloodied.

Edgar picked up the note on his desk and hid it away in a drawer.

"I can't help you. I'm sorry, but I can't help you right now. You're going to have to help yourself. It's better that way."

Martin turned to leave without saying a word. Edgar stared at the boy's retreating back.

"Wait."

Martin stopped and turned around.

"Listen. Listen to this, Martin. Just listen."

Edgar picked up the book and read aloud: "A victim of crime might take note that this crime has transformed him. This is a nonlinear transformation. These transformations move the crime victim from highly organized behavior to seemingly complete chaos."

Edgar closed the book and laid it down.

"You see what that means, don't you? For you and me? Complete chaos. We're lost."

Edgar looked down at the book in front of him as though it had turned into a ticking bomb. He slung the book across the room. The pages fluttered frantically in the air, and the book crashed into the aluminum window blinds. It seemed unnaturally loud in the empty room, unspeakably violent coming from Edgar.

"No. Not lost," Martin said. "We're fucked."

50

PUZZLE SOLVED

Edgar took Friday off from school to run errands with Helen. And sort out what they were going to do about their little problem. Not one for dressing down, Edgar wore his usual white button-down shirt with a colorful tie. The skies had been overcast, so he added his London Fog overcoat as well.

First stop was the OB-GYN. In the waiting room, Helen thumbed through a *Woman's Day* magazine, and Edgar fiddled with his Rubik's Cube. He wasn't really thinking about the puzzle. He was thinking about nothing. The cube seemed to calm him—a baby's pacifier. It kept his mind blank. And the act of not focusing was giving him focus. Almost like an outside observer, Edgar could see himself manipulating the cube, and he vaguely realized that he was actually starting to get the hang of it now. His movements sped up, and the colors on one side of the cube had started to converge and line up. Pretty simple, Edgar thought, when you just looked at it as a whole. Front and back. Right and left. Up and down. All at the same time. But really, he now saw, that wasn't quite right either. The trick was not to color in each of the six faces of the cube, no, you had to look at it like a cake. *Layers.* The secret was layers. He was coming out of himself now, actively participating. He was manipulating the puzzle frantically, his fingers a blur, and the colored squares continued to line up, one after another.

Yes, like putting together a layer cake. Blue, orange, green, and red built in layers. Yellow on the bottom. White icing on top. Puzzle solved.

The nurse called them back to the exam room.

The image was fuzzy and black-and-white, but it was clearly a fetus.

The obstetrician slid the ultrasound paddle in small circles through the conducting gel smeared on Helen's swollen middle. She and Edgar watched with breathless interest.

"Everything looks fine. I don't see anything to give me concern. Perhaps you should stay away from swimming pools until after the delivery."

"You're positive?"

"Positive. She's fine."

* * *

Edgar tossed the solved Rubik's Cube into the glove box before pulling the car out of the parking lot.

"I have my retirement, the 401(k)," he said.

"It'll never be enough."

"I'll sell the house."

"It'll never be enough. I'll go to jail. It'll never be enough and I'll go to jail."

"Maybe not. I told you—"

"No, I left the scene. It was hit-and-run. No matter what you tell them, it was hit-and-run. I was driving drunk. I can't lie about that. I was involved in an accident that resulted in a death. I fled the scene. End of story."

Even though he was driving, Edgar found himself wanting to grab the Rubik's Cube back out of the glove compartment. He wanted to just hold it. It would calm his nerves.

"Are you sure you don't have at least some idea as to what this man's name might be?"

"No. If I ever knew it, it's gone now."

"I can find him. I know I can. I can find him and I can—"

"And you can what?"

"I can find him and . . . I don't know what. I'll fuck him up."

"You'll fuck him up? Edgar, when did you start using the word *fuck*?"

Edgar shrugged. "It's chaos. Mad fuckery."

The businesses along the main strip were starting to thin out as they approached the residential section and their neighborhood. Off to the right Helen saw the Walgreens that she frequently used because of its proximity.

"That day. That day at the drugstore. I think they arrested him for shoplifting. There would be a record of that."

The librarian sat Edgar and Helen at a microfiche terminal and gave them a thick little packet of microfiche sheets. Edgar told her that he already knew how to use the machine.

The *Mantissa Cove Lighthouse*, the local paper, published a daily police blotter. The police blotter was somewhat notorious in that it published mug shots with the crime blurbs. Many folks felt that it unjustly painted the innocent-until-proven-guilty as very much guilty in the court of public opinion. The publisher had doubled circulation in the first month of providing this somewhat unwholesome public service.

The blotter archive was fully searchable online for a modest registration fee, but Edgar felt that it was perhaps wiser to not leave electronic footprints. He was old school, so to speak, and knew that there were ways other than the Internet.

But old school was a great deal more time-consuming. However, since they essentially knew the time frame, it should have been a quick task. But it wasn't. Helen clearly remembered the date, and they thoroughly scanned each item two weeks before that date and two weeks after. There was nothing that struck Helen as a possibility.

"Maybe shoplifting isn't a big enough offense to make the paper," Edgar said. Indeed, the vast majority of the reported arrests were associated with DUI or drug possession and selling, with a smattering of domestic violence thrown in.

"Let's keep looking. We don't have anywhere else to look."

And so Edgar scrolled through the endless parade of local miscreants and their misdeeds. The microfiche film had to be manually changed every ten minutes or so. And it was easy to scroll too fast, causing the images to streak and blur. It was giving Helen a headache. And her back hurt. She just wanted to go. And was about to tell Edgar so when something caught her eye. He had gone back three years when an image struck a chord.

"Stop. Back up a little."

Helen leaned in and studied a photograph of a man alongside a paragraph listing his DUI charge. The man in the photograph had blond hair, not black. There was no scar on his forehead. And he was displaying a tooth-filled smile for the camera as though this were a yearbook photo rather than a mug shot.

But it was him. She was certain. Mr. Slick-Back.

The brief paragraph next to the photo identified him as Cornell Smith of Mantissa County, gave his age, and the charge against him. Driving under the influence of alcohol.

Edgar printed out a copy of the page. Helen folded it and put it in her purse.

Back in the car, headed for home. Helen took off her sweater, balled it up, and placed it between the seat and her lower back to ease the discomfort she was feeling. She settled in and studied the photograph of Cornell Smith. Edgar looked over to her and saw a faint discoloration on her arm where her shirtsleeve had ridden up. He reached over and pushed the sleeve farther up, and saw that her upper arm was dotted with dime-size smudges. Fingertip-shape bruises. They were now faded to a weak rusty orange color.

Helen jerked away, pulling her sleeve back down, and her shame told him everything.

Anger contorted Edgar's face. He snatched the photo of Cornell out of Helen's hand and crumpled it in his fist. He tossed it on the floorboard.

Something on the other side of the street caught Edgar's attention. He twisted the steering wheel and did a quick U-turn. He pulled the car into a parking space in front of the same pawnshop where Helen had sold the ring and he had later met the detectives.

"Just wait here a minute, okay?"

"Fine. What are you doing?"

"I just need for you to wait here. Will you do that?"

Helen nodded her acquiescence, and Edgar got out of the car.

Helen retrieved the balled-up printout from the floorboard—with the considerable effort of bending over her protruding belly. She uncrumpled the paper and studied the photo, willing her mind to remember more about the night she met Cornell Smith. All she could retrieve were flashes of broken images.

She looked out the window trying to see what Edgar was up to, but the reflection was too strong to see inside the pawnshop.

She directed her attention back to the photo, again willing her mind to remember, but it wasn't working. She opened the glove box and saw Edgar's completed Rubik's Cube, and couldn't help but smile. She pushed it to the side and found a black ball-point pen in what was quite possibly the only well-organized glove box in America.

Lightly at first, Helen stroked the pen over the light hair in Cornell's mug shot photograph. She liked the effect and began coloring the hair in heavy dark strokes. The results made the man look more like the Cornell she remembered but didn't jog any additional memories.

She looked around again for any sign of Edgar, but there was none. She smoothed and folded the printout and got out of the car.

From the sidewalk, Helen peered through the window of the pawnshop and saw Edgar standing at the sales counter. He was holding a gun, admiring it. It was huge, looked like a movie prop. Like something Dirty Harry would carry. Edgar nodded in approval and handed the weapon back to the pawnbroker.

A flurry of images swirled through Helen's mind. Of Edgar the puzzle solver, of Edgar the Christmas tree topper, of Edgar the neat freak. And now this gentle man was buying a gun to perpetrate violence. And, at the heart of it all, the knowledge that it was she who had brought him to this point. She was responsible.

When Helen walked inside, Edgar was filling out paperwork and the pawnbroker was saying, "License, permit, background check. You're gonna—"

Helen spoke over him in a calm but final voice. "No. No. No."

She reached over gently but firmly and took the permit application away from Edgar.

"No."

51

DEAR, YOU HAVE A VISITOR

The creased and drawn-on printout of Cornell's police blotter photo was taped to a sheet of chart paper over Edgar's desk. Edgar had started three columns on the chart:

WHAT WE KNOW.
WHAT HE KNOWS.
WHAT WE NEED TO KNOW.

Helen stared at the chart. Charts she could handle, but where would this lead them? Back to the pawnshop for a gun?

She scrolled through the contacts list on her cell phone but remembered that she had deleted that number long ago. It didn't matter. She dialed the number from memory. It rang five times, then went to voice mail.

"I need you. I'm not going to drink, but I need you. I need your help. Edgar is . . . Oh Martha . . . Edgar . . . He tried to buy a gun. Edgar. A gun. And I hope you do break people's fingers. I hope you are a criminal. Please be a criminal and help us—"

Helen ended the call when she heard Edgar emerging from the bedroom. He passed her on his way to the kitchen.

"I don't see how we'll ever find him," she said to Edgar's back. "Or what the point would be. Maybe we should talk to a private investigator. Or a lawyer. Or Martha. That's what she does. Finds people."

Edgar emerged from the kitchen reading from the phone book.

"Cornell Smith, seventeen thirty-five Finney Road." Old school triumphed yet again.

"Oh. You're so thorough."

Edgar put down the phone book and picked up his keys.

"I'm going to see him."

"And do what? Thorough him to death? Thorough him into leaving us alone?"

"I think I'll just ask him how bruises in the shape of his fingers ended up on my wife's arm."

"If I turn myself in, it can be manslaughter. Seven years. I can be out in seven years."

"You're due in two weeks. Two weeks—"

Helen talked over him. "Seven years. She will still be young.

Young enough that she might not even remember later. Maybe even less than seven years. With a good lawyer. I checked. Then we'll be clean."

"No. Never. That's unacceptable. I lost a lifetime already. I won't risk seven years."

"It's the only way. It's the ninth step. Make amends. I have to make amends."

Edgar brushed past her.

"I'm going to see him. I'll buy him off. I don't know what will happen. Maybe he needs to make amends too. Maybe I can help him. Or maybe I'll just put my fucking foot up his ass."

Helen grabbed his arm to hold him back, but Edgar pulled away.

The doorbell rang, and Edgar stormed to the door. He yanked it open to find the last person in the world he expected to see standing on his front porch. Cornell Smith.

"Hi there. Is Helen home?

Without missing a beat, Edgar said, "Just one minute," and closed the door.

Edgar ripped the Cornell chart off the wall, wadded it up, and tossed it into the trash.

He called out to Helen: "Dear, you have a visitor."

52

AN INVESTMENT OPPORTUNITY

Edgar peeked in on Cornell from the kitchen while Helen prepared coffee.

A light sparked in Edgar's eyes, giving him a wild, almost
unhinged look. He was running on adrenaline, and he seemed
almost giddy. To Helen, he appeared to be on the edge of losing
control.

Conversely, Helen was subdued and calm and seemed more
sure of herself than ever before.

Edgar whispered to Helen, "Just pretend."

Helen shook her head—more in disgust than refusal.

"Just let him think that I still don't know. Let him think that
it's the same as before. That he's got the upper hand. That
you're scared. You can do that, right? Be scared?"

"And what are you going to do?" Helen hissed. "Call the police? Do it or I will. I mean it."

Edgar poked his head out of the kitchen and called out.

"Uh, Cornell, we're just gonna make a fresh pot of coffee."

"That's mighty decent of you, old sport."

Edgar stared at him, then shrugged.

"Just pretend," Edgar pleaded one last time as he grabbed the coffee tray and headed out with it.

"So you two grew up together?"

"We surely did. We were always close. Weren't we, Helen?"

Helen was loath to join in this charade. Her head might have nodded in agreement, but then again it might not have.

The three of them sipped their coffee in an interlude of keenly uncomfortable silence. Helen's cell phone rang. She reached into her purse, silencing it.

Edgar asked, "And what did you say brought you out today, Cornell?"

As though Cornell had been waiting all along to be asked this very question, his demeanor took on a humble cast and he leaned forward as though speaking in the strictest of confidence.

"Well, Edgar, I guess . . . I guess when an old friend turns up unannounced as I have today, it's usually because they need some kind of help."

Edgar cleared his throat. "Is that right?"

"I'm afraid so."

"Speak your mind, Cornell."

"I thank you for saying that. Truth is, I'm looking for investors. I need to raise—"

Edgar snapped his fingers.

"Hold that thought. I'll be right back."

Edgar left the living room and went upstairs.

Cornell stared at Helen.

"You didn't think I'd do it, did you?"

Helen shook her head, speechless.

"I don't want to mess up your life. But I will. I'll ruin everything. All you have to do is get him to invest in my business deal. When I disappear with the money, your husband will just think you were conned. He'll never know."

Edgar rummaged through the medicine cabinet in his bathroom. Bottles fell and scattered as he picked through them. At last he found the expired bottle of Xanax that had been prescribed to him to treat his anxiety after Judy's death. He'd never actually taken any, so the bottle still held the full prescribed amount.

Edgar pocketed the bottle and headed back downstairs.

Crossing the living room, he asked Cornell, "How'd you like a little something-something to perk up that coffee?" And even gave Cornell a sly wink.

"I believe I'd like that just fine."

In the kitchen, Edgar found a soup bowl and dumped about half of the Xanax in it. Applying pressure with his thumb, he used the back of a spoon to crush the blue oval tablets. Then he dug out the bottle of commemorative brandy from the bottom cabinet. He broke the seal and poured some of the brandy into the sink. He made a funnel shape with one hand and poured the ground Xanax into the brandy bottle. Edgar capped it and shook the concoction until he was sure the grainy powder had dissolved.

"Here we go," he said to Cornell, "just the thing." He poured a healthy dollop into Cornell's coffee.

"Oh, we go way back."

Cornell was greatly relaxed and took no notice that he was the only one partaking of the brandy.

"Do tell."

"Fact is, and not to make you uncomfortable, but we courted as teenagers. Remember that, Helen?"

Helen refused to respond.

"Well, no point in digging up the past, is there, Helen? Some things that's buried should stay buried."

"That sounds ominous."

Cornell pushed his cup toward Edgar.

"You can skip the coffee."

Edgar loaded him up, and Cornell drained the cup, wiping the last drop from his chin.

"Thanks, old sport. Now, I hate to say this, Edgar, Helen, but like I said, I have a reason for looking you up. It's uncomfortable to say, but I need a loan. Well, no, not a loan. I didn't mean to say that. It's an investment opportunity."

Edgar refilled Cornell's cup and said, "Money can ruin a friendship."

"We wasn't never that close nohow," Cornell said, and then burped. He was beginning to sway like a bowling pin.

"It's up to Helen. I support her in whatever she chooses to do."

Helen shook her head and said, "I don't want anything to do with any of this."

Cornell peered imperiously down at Helen through slitted eyes.

"That just ain't gonna work."

Edgar appeared to be giving the matter careful consideration. He said, "Well, how about this, Cornell? How about we tie you up, kill you, and bury you in the backyard?"

"Edgar!"

Cornell cocked his eyebrow as though mulling over that proposal, then slumped forward onto the floor.

53

NOBODY KNOWS ABOUT
STUFF LIKE THIS

The house was unnaturally quiet. Edgar and Helen stared at each other over their blackmailer's unconscious body.

What now?

As if in answer to that unspoken question, shrill electronic music broke the silence in the living room. Edgar and Helen exchanged a curious look as the theme from *The Sting* played over and over.

Edgar uncrumpled Cornell's slumped body and went through his pockets until he found the cell phone. He held it up to show Helen, then shoved it back into Cornell's pocket without answering it. It finally stopped ringing.

The doorbell rang, followed by an urgent knock on the front door.

"You gotta be fucking kidding me," Edgar said.

"Let me—"

"Shhhh, maybe they'll go away."

But the knocking and ringing continued. Insistent. Then a faint voice that they both recognized as Martha's: "Hello! Helen? Helen?"

"Just ignore her."

"She knows we're home. Our cars are out there. And so is Cornell's."

"Helen? Are you okay? Helen!"

"For the love of Christ."

Helen got up, but Edgar motioned her back down.

"Maybe she can help us. She knows about stuff like this."

"Nobody knows about stuff like this."

"But—"

"No!"

They could now see Martha trying to peer in through the front window, cupping her hands to block out the horizontal glare of the setting sun.

Edgar went to the door and opened it. Martha was standing off to the side in an azalea bed, still peering through the window. She looked up, startled.

"You *are* home."

"Martha, now is not a good time. You can call—"

"I'm afraid I must insist. I have to speak to Helen."

"She's not home."

"She just called me. And her car's right there."

"True. But can't people go places without their cars?"

"Typically, no."

"A friend picked her up."

"Her friend appears to have left his or her car here as well."

Martha had made her way out of the azalea bed and back up the front porch. She tried to glance through the open door into the house, but Edgar had it blocked.

"That's *my* friend's car."

"Oh. Well, be a dear and let me use the bathroom before I go."

Edgar didn't budge.

"I'm going to soil myself. You know I have bowel issues. Don't tell me you're going to stand there and let an old lady shit her pants right before your very eyes?"

"Look, Martha, I'm going to level with you. This is . . . I shouldn't have to explain myself. Helen. She probably called you because she found out I'm having an affair. She's upset. It's personal. Private."

"I want to see her."

"Now is not the time."

"I believe it is. And whose car is that in the driveway?"

Edgar looked again at Cornell's beat-up Volvo looking out of place.

He didn't know what else to say, so Edgar said, "Fuck off!" and slammed the door.

Not looking very happy, Martha got back in her car and drove away. Once she was out of the neighborhood, she turned around and drove back in.

She parked a safe distance from the house.

Watching. Worried.

54

HE LEVELED THE GUN AT CORNELL'S HEAD

The last of the day's sunlight cast weak, slender beams through gaps in the curtains. Helen sat across from Cornell's supine body while Edgar paced.

Nylon cord bound Cornell at the wrists, ankles, and thighs. Mitzi licked his stubbly face, and Molly had curled up in the warmth of his stomach.

"You've got him trussed up like the Christmas goose. What now?"

"We have to check his house. He might have something there. Something that incriminates us. And his car is in our driveway."

"I'm not going to let you hurt him."

"I have no intention of hurting anybody."

"Then what are you going to do?"

"I don't know yet, but we've got to get him out of here."

The headlights of Cornell's Volvo illuminated only what was directly in front of Edgar. All else was hidden in the dark. In the rearview mirror, Edgar checked on Helen following behind them in Edgar's vehicle.

Cornell was in the backseat, the seat belt doing little to hold him up. He was starting to regain a degree of consciousness. He was too big for Edgar to carry alone, and Helen was too pregnant to help carry him, so they removed the cord from his legs and waited until Cornell could be roused enough to stagger to the car with Edgar's support.

Cornell's cell phone rang again, and the familiar notes of "The Entertainer" filled the car. Edgar looked at Cornell in the rearview mirror.

"Want me to get that? Tell them you're tied up right now?"

Edgar was wearing gloves. He didn't let Helen see him bring the gloves. Something told him it would be best to leave no fingerprints.

Finney Road was on the undeveloped outskirts of Mantissa County. Mobile homes dotted the roadside, some set back in the pines, some just a few feet off the road.

At 1735 Finney Road sat Cornell Smith's dilapidated trailer with its stolen electricity and hacked satellite TV. Edgar draped a coat over Cornell's bound wrists and assisted Cornell into the trailer. Cornell was groggy but awake. Helen struggled along behind them.

Edgar stumbled over the threshold and his glasses flew from his face as he struggled to keep both himself and Cornell from falling. He shoved Cornell onto the unmade bed and retrieved his glasses from the corner. He inspected them and saw that the left lens was horizontally cracked, but still functional. He and Helen looked around at the general shabbiness of the place. Cornell was aware of what was happening but still very much subdued. He gave no indication of protest or fight.

Edgar set about searching the trailer. He was determined to make a thorough job of it. He wanted to know what Cornell knew. To see if there was physical evidence of any kind.

Helen plopped onto the couch, very pregnant and very tired. She watched Edgar go about his search, and she thought that in his white shirt, tie, and black overcoat, he looked like an FBI agent.

"I do want to say that drugging me was—"

"I need for you to not talk."

Edgar's tone clearly communicated that now was not the time for discourse or bargaining.

Helen asked, "What are you looking for?"

"Anything that links him to you. To us."

"Why? What does it matter? Are you going kill him?" That pierced Cornell's brain, and roused him to full attention. "If not, then what's the point? There could be something hidden. Something that you could never find. You'll never be sure."

Helen took a deep breath. She was cramping. But she knew that it wasn't a real cramp. That it was a contraction. Her water had broken during the car ride. She'd cleaned herself up with fast-food napkins from the glove box. But she didn't want to tell Edgar. Not yet. If there was any way that this could all come to some kind of conclusion tonight, then she would find a way to will the labor to slow down. She didn't see how this could end in a good way, but she believed in Edgar's decency. She believed in his intelligence. If there was a solution, she believed he could find it. He just needed to take a breath and get back on a good path.

"And why? What are you thinking, Edgar? Stop yourself. Stop yourself and think."

Cornell offered, "What if I told you—"

"Shut up!"

Edgar was pulling out kitchen drawers and emptying them on the floor. Utensils scattered and piled up. He opened the last drawer and paused. He reached in and pulled out a gun.

He leveled the gun at Cornell's head.

Helen cried out—both in protest and at the pain of a fresh contraction. Edgar looked at her, and the cracked lens of his bifocals made him look unstable, off-kilter. She truly had no idea what he would do next.

Edgar cocked the gun.

"Do you have anything here that links you to us?"

"No. Nothing."

"What do you suggest we do? What's the solution here?"

"Let me go. I'll never tell. Never."

"Because I can only think of one solution. I won't let you rob me of my life. I'll not be a victim. Not again."

"Edgar, think! Stop and think."

"Just listen. You don't have to worry about me. She didn't kill your wife."

"What?"

"She didn't kill your wife. I did."

55

EVEN STEVEN

"How do you think I lost my teeth? Got this scar? Helen, you saw the hole in your windshield. It was my head that put it there, not yours. I drove your car. You don't have to worry about me. I don't have anything on you. I'm sorry, Helen."

"I wasn't driving?"

"No. I took your keys. I drove your car. You're not a bad person, Helen. I am."

And with that bit of information, her body stopped fighting the labor contractions. It was as though her mind told her body, *Okay, we got what we wanted. Have at it.*

"Edgar, we have to go. The baby is coming."

But Edgar didn't hear her. He was lost in his own revelation. And when he did look up, it was at Cornell he looked, not

233

Helen. He pressed the bore of the gun dead center to Cornell's forehead.

"You just admitted to killing my wife. What makes you think I won't end your life right here, right now?"

"Cause you're not a killer. If you were, you'da killed me two hours ago." He held his bound hands out to Edgar. "Let me go. I don't have anything on you."

"Let him go, Edgar. We're clean. Free. The baby is coming. I have to get to the hospital right now."

Edgar relaxed the gun. He put it in his pocket. "He's a drunk. A blackmailer. A bully." Edgar reached forward and took a cigarette from the pack in Cornell's breast pocket. "A murderer." He put the cigarette in Cornell's mouth. "He needs to make amends."

He struck a match. Cornell gulped the smoke gratefully. Edgar held on to the lit match.

"He has sedatives and alcohol in his system. That's what the autopsy would show. No one would ever think twice."

Edgar dropped the burning match into the tangled bed covers. It guttered, seemed to go out, and then a weak flame took hold.

Helen struggled to find the exact words, to get through to Edgar. "It will eat at your soul."

Edgar started the car and looked forward at the trailer. The flames were dancing, licking, and writhing. The yellow light caught in the cracked left lens of his glasses.

Next to him, Helen had her eyes closed in pain.

And in the backseat, Cornell Smith was bound at the wrists, ankles, and thighs—very much alive.

In the end, Edgar just didn't have it in him to murder a man.

"Just take me to the police. I'll turn myself in."

"Do it, Edgar. Do something. I'm going to have this baby right fucking now."

"We can't. You weren't driving, but you covered up a crime."

"Then let me go. Let me out right here. I won't tell. You got something on me. I got something on you. Even steven. You'll never see me again. Never."

Edgar found the gloppy mess of fast-food napkins, wet with amniotic fluid, and shoved them into Cornell's mouth. He pushed Cornell to the floor and threw a coat over him.

"Hospital. Please, Edgar. Hospital."

Edgar burned rubber.

56

THE CORNELL PROBLEM

He took Helen in through the emergency entrance, and once she had been admitted, Edgar removed the car from the emergency drop-off. He parked the car on the most deserted level of the parking deck he could find. He checked on Cornell. The ropes were still secure, and the napkins were still wadded into his mouth. Edgar wished he had some duct tape to put over Cornell's mouth, but he didn't. The napkins would have to do. He found a gray emergency blanket stowed away with the spare tire and flare kit. He used this to make sure Cornell stayed completely hidden. During all of this, Cornell grunted and tried to gain Edgar's attention, but Edgar would not make eye contact with the man.

Edgar had decided on some level to compartmentalize the Cornell problem. He sealed it off to be dealt with at a later time.

He went back to the hospital to see his daughter being born.

The delivery was quick and without complication. Textbook, the OB said. Within three hours of being admitted, Edgar and Helen were new parents and had been placed in a room on the maternity ward. The sun had risen on a bright day, and their daughter, Isabella, slept soundly in the clear plastic crib between them.

There was a cushioned perch built onto the windowsill for husbands to rest and sleep. And that was what Edgar did. He slept. His sleep was untroubled. His problems had been neatly compartmentalized, and they could not reach him.

The day passed in a series of moments of wakefulness and sleep. Nurses and attendants wandered in and out of the room, monitoring Helen and whisking Isabella away for different blood tests, screenings, and immunizations. Sometimes Edgar would waken and change Isabella's diaper and feed her a bottle while Helen slept. Sometimes, Helen would feed Isabella from her breast while Edgar slept. When they were awake together, they would marvel over Isabella's tininess, her perfect fingers, her pink toes.

Late in the day, the charge nurse said that they would likely be discharged the following day.

"That quick?" Helen asked.

"Twenty-four to forty-eight hours is the norm for vaginal deliveries with no complications."

"Wow. That's great."

But, of course, it wasn't great. Helen too had compartmentalized, and she knew that her discharge would signal the end of this reprieve. By tacit design, she and Edgar had not spoken of the incidents leading up to this moment. She did not want to know. She only wanted to be a mother.

That night, Edgar kissed Helen's head and said he needed to take care of a few things. That she should call him as soon as her discharge came through.

57

LAYERS

It was four A.M., Monday morning. Dawn was not yet even a hint. But it would be soon. Edgar had just left downtown, where he had visited an ATM, and now he drove along the scenic highway. He had driven for hours before he could force himself to open that inner compartment, but once he did, he found the solution to his problem alarmingly simple. Cornell had said it himself. Even steven. He had something on them, but they also had something on him. Even steven. He wasn't a threat. He would always be an uncertainty. A dark shadow. But he wasn't a threat.

Under the blanket in the back of the car, Cornell had not been forced to compartmentalize. He had been hard at work over the last twenty-four hours focusing purely on saving his own life. He had become certain that Edgar was going to kill him. It only stood to reason.

He had spit out the soggy napkins easily enough and used his teeth to see what he could do about the ropes. It was slow going without his two front teeth. He had dozed off a few times, but he had more or less concentrated on breaking his bindings. What else was there for him to do?

Edgar drove to the Greyhound depot. The bus station itself was quite modest, but adjoining it was the regional storage and repair hub with a sprawling parking area where hundreds of buses were put out for repair; most of them appeared forgotten. Edgar pulled his car into the deserted storage field, hidden among the monolithic buses.

Under the blanket, Cornell was at work. From the moment the car had cranked up and gotten back on the road, he had redoubled his efforts to free himself from the ropes. He had been using his bottom teeth as a sort of saw, back and forth, back and forth with the serrated tops of his remaining central incisors. But the cords were nylon or some other synthetic material. Each thread was a monumental struggle, but about twenty minutes earlier, Cornell had cut through the last strand, freeing his hands. It took ten minutes for even a small bit of feeling to return to them so that he could—cautiously—reach down and try to free the knots that bound his thighs and ankles. But he could not work his swollen, benumbed fingers into the tight knots.

Nonetheless, he had freed his hands. He could at least defend himself.

And now the car had stopped.

What would happen next?

Edgar took out his wallet and retrieved the cash he had withdrawn from the ATM. One thousand dollars was the daily limit.

He opened the glove compartment (even in his current state, Edgar noted that the contents were in disarray, with a jumble of fast-food napkins and the Rubik's Cube tossed in there as well) and rummaged under the title papers to see if there might be an envelope. There wasn't, so he smoothed out several paper napkins and folded them over the money, making a relatively neat package. He extracted a pen and wrote (squinting through the cracked left lens) on the package: *As far as it will take you. Last chance.*

His plan was to not even speak to Cornell, but simply untie him and hand him the money. After replacing the pen in the glove compartment, Edgar picked up the Rubik's Cube. He kissed it like a good-luck charm.

That was when Cornell exploded from the backseat. An explosion of fear and violence, attacking Edgar.

With Cornell having the advantage of surprise, Edgar didn't stand a chance. Cornell had flipped himself over the seat back and come down on top of Edgar with the full force of his body.

The weight of Cornell's still-bound lower body pinned Edgar. Cornell had his hands wrapped around Edgar's neck, throttling him full strength, with every intention of squeezing the life out of him.

"Your cunt wife's going to jail," Cornell hissed through teeth clenched in exertion. "And you're going to hell."

Cornell tightened his grip even more, squeezing, squeezing, squeezing. Edgar's face puffed in an angry red, then faded to a complacent blue.

Edgar didn't actually remember the Rubik's Cube still clenched in his clawed hand; he was really only convulsing when he brought the hand up and then down in a wicked arc. The protruding corner of the cube connected viciously with Cornell's temple.

Cornell's grip around Edgar's neck lessened, and air rushed inside his screaming lungs. The atavistic thing that Edgar had become did not truly understand what it had done, only that the last action had brought relief. So the action was repeated. The cube slammed into Cornell's head. Again. And again.

Stunned and bleeding, Cornell managed the door handle and spilled out of the car onto the asphalt, his bound legs, like a useless serpentine appendage, tumbling behind him. A wounded animal, he crawled (well, slithered) to the closest shelter. Under the bus, Cornell gathered himself. Watched and waited.

What would happen next?

The Ninth Step

* * *

Edgar sat in the car, looking at the Rubik's Cube, the smeared blood, and the single strand of jet-black hair caught in a groove.

Edgar stepped out of the car.

The depot was bathed in blackness; the sodium arc lights on the outskirts backlit the rows of buses so that it felt like a shadow maze of high walls.

Edgar stood and listened. And watched. There was no sign of Cornell. Edgar stepped forward. The cube, grasped loosely in his hand, dangled at his side. *Layers*, he thought. *Layers*. The gritty sound of his steady footsteps was all that could be heard in the maze of buses.

Edgar got down on his hands and knees and began looking under the vehicles. The lot lights actually threw more light under the buses than between them. He went from bus to bus, methodic, searching. And he spotted Cornell tucked behind a dry rotted tire.

Edgar didn't hesitate. He dove under the bus and lunged forward, reaching for Cornell, but Cornell reacted, his cocooned legs jacking out; he didn't make contact but did manage to kick Edgar's glasses off his face. Edgar recoiled, smashing his head on the metal undercarriage. He heard his glasses skittering behind him, sliding off into the murky darkness. Without his glasses he was damn near blind, but he dared not stop to find them now.

He stayed on the offensive, moving forward. Using his ears

to guide him, Edgar crawled farther under the bus, listening for the slithering sound Cornell made as he retreated. Cornell was no more than a blur to Edgar, but he pursued him with a single-minded savagery.

Cornell scooted and pulled himself forward, clawing at the pavement, ripping off fingernails in his desperation. From one bus to the next he clawed his way forward, just out of Edgar's reach. Until there were no buses left. Cornell emerged and saw an open expanse of scrub grass with highway lights twinkling in the distance. He paused to gather himself, to decide what to do next. But that pause cost him everything. He felt Edgar's hand grip his ankle like the unyielding talon of a bird of prey.

Edgar pulled Cornell back under the bus. Cornell grabbed at the pavement, losing more fingernails, but he could not beat the force drawing him under.

Edgar pulled Cornell back inside the walled maze. On his knees, Edgar positioned himself over Cornell and watched him try yet again to wriggle away, his lower body dragging behind. Edgar turned him over as one would a scurrying bug, flipping him onto his back and immobilizing him. Cornell looked into Edgar's eyes and saw a vacancy there, a lack of self-awareness, and realized all was lost.

Game over, old sport.

Cornell closed his eyes and said, "God damn."

After the first blow, Cornell cried out, but Edgar did not hear those cries for mercy. He repeatedly brought the cube down on Cornell's head.

One savage blow after another. *Layers.*

Like a caricature of a blind man, Edgar patted the cold asphalt surface, feeling for his glasses. Without them he would not be able to drive his car. In his mind's eye, he imagined his hands coming within millimeters of his glasses, but never actually touching them. But such was not his fate, and after five minutes of fruitless crawling and searching, his hand came squarely down on the bifocals. The left lens still bore its single horizontal hairline crack, but the right was now smashed to an opaque cataract. But the left side was enough for him to be able to see, to do what still needed to be done.

Rather than drag Cornell's body through the landscape of bus carcasses, Edgar drove the car through the ranks, stopping beside Cornell's supine body, Cornell's eyes staring skyward in a final look of surprise.

Moving a human body, Edgar quickly learned, was not an easy task. After lining the bottom of the trunk with the emergency blanket (to catch any blood, or other DNA evidence—modern forensics was a force to be reckoned with, and Edgar made a mental note to vacuum the entire car with a public vacuum and spray the trunk with bleach solution), Edgar found that the simple mechanics of transferring the body from the ground to the trunk were beyond his physical capabilities. It wasn't the weight of the body; it was the complete lack of resistance. No matter how he tried to scoop up Cornell, the corpse just slipped out of his grasp. Slipped *through* his grasp. Errant limbs went askew. The head lolled as though tethered by only a string. The torso had no more consistency than a strand of limp spaghetti. It was impossible.

At one point, in midlift, the body shifted in such a way that it nearly toppled Edgar. He had to simultaneously drop it and reach overhead to grab the trunk lid to keep from falling on top of the body. When he let go of the trunk lid, Edgar did not realize that he had left a single, perfect thumbprint delineated in Cornell's blood. As Edgar was learning, when it came to committing a crime—and getting away with it—there were an untold number of variables. This was one he did not catch.

Edgar eyed the blanket lining the trunk and was struck by inspiration. He spread the blanket (not a big one, but just big enough, he reckoned) beside the body. It took only three moves to get the body onto the blanket: first the head and shoulders, then the feet and legs, and then it was a simple matter of grabbing hold of the belt and shifting the remainder of the torso atop the blanket. Layers seemed to be the solution to many of life's little problems. With the body atop the blanket, it would be no more difficult than folding a burrito. A very large, very heavy burrito.

Before making the first fold, Edgar saw an angular irregularity in the otherwise chaotic pulp that he had beaten Cornell's head into. He leaned in and studied the protruding corner. Then he reached down and plucked the section of the Rubik's Cube (the section itself a minicube with a little protruding arm that interlocked with the other minicubes) that was lodged in Cornell's temple. *No wonder criminals are so often caught*, Edgar thought. *So many variables to contain.*

And his mind was just not working as it normally did. If Edgar had to use just one word to describe his usual thought process, it would be *organized*. And now, tonight, just when he needed that quality most of all, it had seemingly deserted him. Thoughtless emotion had taken over. *No*, Edgar realized. *Not emotion. Instinct. Like an animal.* But animals, animals that guided themselves by instinct alone, did not pause to give concern to being caught. He decided to slow down, to bring back organized thought. He needed to be thorough.

Edgar got back on his hands and knees and started searching. He could see now, at least partially, so he quickly found the Rubik's Cube under the adjoining bus. *The murder weapon. Had he really almost left behind the murder weapon?* He saw that there was only the one missing section, and he snapped that piece back into the cube. He also noted with curiosity that the beating he'd administered had somehow dislodged the puzzle from its completed position. The cube was now unsolved. A part of Edgar wanted to complete the few twists it would have taken to once again line up all the colors, but he recognized that as an idiotic impulse and didn't give in to it. He tucked the cube next to the body and finished rolling it up.

The nylon cord was still in the backseat, so Edgar trussed up his Taco Bell Burrito Supreme with special Rubik's Cube sauce with three lengths of the rope. He was then able to manhandle the body by grasping the cords and heaving it up to, and into, the trunk.

Edgar looked down at his handiwork and was greeted with the sound of music. Doo-dee doo-doo doo-doo doo-doo; doo-dee dee-dee dee-dee dee-dee deeeeee. "The Entertainer." Cornell's phone chirped clear as a bell even through the blanket.

Who in the fuck kept calling? Edgar decided that there was no way he was going cut the cords and unwrap his Mexican treat to silence the phone. That was a layer he was just going to have to let go. He was too tired, and it wasn't worth the effort.

He closed the trunk with a deliberate, vacillation–ending assuredness. A few final chords of "The Entertainer" could plainly be heard in the quiet storage depot. Then silence. Blessed silence. He had done it.

That was when he remembered the gun. Yet another layer. He had Cornell's gun in his coat pocket. *My God, the variables!* He should have wrapped that up with the body as well. Now that bit of business was probably worth unwrapping the burrito, but Edgar felt that he'd been here far too long. He thought of small changes in ordinary variables. Internal and external variables. Of nonlinear transformations in the behavior of complex systems. He imagined people as lines moving at random, moving in chaos, and thought of the path of one line intersecting with the path on which his line had taken him.

He needed to keep his line moving.

Edgar looked to the heavens and said, "God damn."

He got in the car and drove away, the bloody thumbprint on the back of the trunk a stark exclamation point.

58

THE FORGOTTEN CLUE

Edgar drove. The hum of the engine pacified his jangled nerves. Dawn had given way to morning. And still Edgar drove. Going nowhere. School buses and early commuters were beginning to show up on the roads.

His mind replayed the last two days' events over and over, searching for bits of evidence he might have overlooked. He was positive there was something, but he just could not quite grasp hold of it.

He had stopped at a gas station and spent thirty minutes in the restroom cleaning himself. His skin and hair were easy enough, and there were just a few stains on his clothes, but the black overcoat had taken most of it, and it didn't really show on the black material. By the time he had finished daubing the spots with liquid soap and scrubbing them with wet paper towels, the stains looked no more menacing than a sloppy spaghetti dinner. During the ablutions, Edgar heard the occasional padded thump of Cornell's gun swaying in his overcoat pocket and banging against the sink. He considered wiping it down and tossing the weapon in the bathroom trash can but decided against it. It seemed risky, and he didn't like the idea of depositing evidence across a wide area. Lines could intersect. Variables grew exponentially. *Layers, my friend. Layers.*

Of the thumbprint on the back of the trunk, however, Edgar remained unaware. It stood out like a scarlet confession, but only to the guilty. To any driver who saw it, it looked like an ordinary smudge. If someone were to take a closer inspection, it might look like a painter's hand had caused a thoughtless mistake. That is, if they were not looking for guilt.

Edgar struggled for insight into his increasingly disorganized thought process and was at last able to admit to himself that there was nothing else. No other evidence. He simply did not know what to do with the body. And rather than admit this, he had latched on to this idea of the unraveled thread. The forgotten clue.

He forced himself to let that idea drop and cast about for options on where to dispose of the body. And the gun. A landfill? That was a thought. But in broad daylight? The body was wrapped up, concealed. So he would only look like any ordinary person dropping off a 180-pound burrito at the town dump.

A roadside ditch? That was pretty ugly. A shallow grave out in the woods? What woods? And what about nonlinear transformations? Intersections? Paths crossed in chaos? He would have to go home and get a shovel. Or stop at a hardware store and buy one. His mind flashed on an image of the imaginary clerk who sold him the shovel sitting on a witness stand, his imaginary finger pointed in accusation at Edgar. *Him, he's the one.* And the prosecutor asking him later, *Please, explain it to us once again, Mr. Woolrich. Tell us why, less than thirty-six hours after your wife gave birth to your daughter, you felt compelled to take a two-hour drive and buy a shovel?*

Edgar willed his mind to organize. To just please organize. But he couldn't. All he could see was that smug imaginary prosecutor lining up the evidence. The errant hair strand or stray microdroplet found in the trunk (you could never get it all). *Do you care to tell us about that, Mr. Woolrich? Just how did a strand of Cornell Smith's hair end up in your trunk? In* your *trunk! And what about this, Mr. Woolrich,* the prosecutor would trumpet, waving a slip of paper in the air. *What about this note found in your desk? Demanding money. Isn't it true that Cornell Smith was blackmailing you?*

The note! That was it. That was what he had forgotten. In his desk at school. Tucked in a drawer so Martin wouldn't see it. And then forgotten.

His mind. What had happened to his mind?

Edgar turned the car around.

59

THE HEAT CLOSING IN

Edgar decided that no matter how much his mind had slipped, he had the God-given sense not to drive on school property with a corpse in his trunk, so he headed first for home. He did indeed have a shovel in the garage, but that would be for later. Whatever he was going to do, he couldn't very well do it in broad daylight. Or gray daylight. It was overcast today.

He would stash Cornell's body in the garage for safekeeping. Just until he could figure out what to do. No, better yet, leave it in the trunk. Just park the car in the garage and take Helen's car to the school. That way, it would save his back from lifting the body again and decrease the chances of cross-contaminating his home with DNA evidence.

The neighborhood was quiet as always, and the calm, familiar atmosphere transferred to Edgar. With a plan (albeit a half-assed one) in place, he was starting to feel some small degree of confidence that he might actually get away with this.

That tranquillity was shattered when Edgar turned onto his street. Immediately, he saw the police cruiser parked in his driveway and adrenaline surged through his body like an electric shock. A lone officer was leaning against the cruiser, speaking into his radio.

How was this possible? Why would a policeman be at his house first thing in the morning? How could they know Cornell was dead? How was that even possible? Were there surveillance cameras at the bus depot? Edgar didn't see how. There would have been no way to power them. The lighting ran only to the outskirts. What was going on? He knew he had to get rid of the body. The police were looking for him. They would search his car. But only if they had a search warrant. Why were they looking for him? Could it possibly be something completely unrelated? Could it? Of course it couldn't.

All of these thoughts shuttled through his mind almost simultaneously. Edgar, the picture of suburban serenity, drove purposefully past his own driveway, looking straight ahead. At the next block, he turned right, then right again, and then he was out of the neighborhood.

He decided to go straight to the school. What else was there to do? He had to have that note. Every strand needed to be gathered. Cauterized. As he pulled out onto the main road, a line from William S. Burroughs occurred to him, popped up unbidden in his mind: *I can feel the heat closing in.* And what was it? *Setting up their devil doll stool pigeons.* He'd read it in college. In those days, it had seemed like every incoming freshman was issued a bong and a copy of *Naked Lunch.* Edgar had passed on the water pipe but gave Burroughs a try. He'd absolutely hated it. The narrative was a disjointed, disorganized mess. He'd forced himself to finish reading it and then passed it off to somebody else. Maybe you had to smoke pot for it to make sense. Edgar simply didn't get it. And he hadn't realized until right now that some of Burroughs's febrile words had left a mark on him. *I can feel the heat closing in, feel them out there making their moves, setting up their devil doll stool pigeons.*

He simply had to retrieve that note. It was the last piece of evidence. The only thing that could cast any suspicion on him or Helen. It was the devil doll stool pigeon waiting to rat him out.

His cell phone rang. It was Helen. She and the baby had been discharged. They were ready whenever he was. Helen didn't ask what he was doing, and Edgar didn't volunteer. An unspoken agreement had passed between them. It was Edgar's responsibility to protect his family. It was Helen's responsibility to not ask questions and allow him to do his job. The primitive act of childbirth, the ancient roles they had each taken on; these things awoke an instinct. A selfish, ruthless survivalism.

* * *

As he made his way down the deserted school hallway, the hair-line fissure on one side of his glasses, and the crackled milk glass of the other, gave Edgar a deranged, unhinged appearance.

The first bell had rung ten minutes ago. Classes were well underway. Edgar had forgotten to call in absent. He would just explain to Cleage that the labor had come on suddenly, and in all the excitement, he'd forgotten to call the school. Cleage would understand. Once he had the note, he might even stop by Cleage's office and apologize. That could be his excuse for being in the building. *I just wanted to tell you we had the baby. A healthy little girl. Yes, thank you. And also, I just wanted to personally stop by and apologize for not calling in. No, not all. I just wanted to tell you in person. In fact, I'm on my way right this minute to pick them up from the hospital. Just needed to run back home and get the child safety seat. You know, they won't let you leave the hospital without one of those.* Yes, yes, yes. How very, very Edgar. Edgar also made a mental note to stop by Wal-Mart and purchase a new child restraint seat since there was no way he was going home to get the one they had already bought.

Edgar stopped at his classroom door, thinking of what he might mutter to whoever was the substitute teacher while he rummaged through his desk for the note. He glanced through the small wire-reinforced glass window set into the door, and his heart stopped. Principal Cleage was standing at his desk, which in itself was not so odd—it was only ten minutes into the day and Edgar had, after all, not alerted anyone to his absence. Cleage was likely covering until the substitute showed up. Yes, that would make sense. What made absolutely no sense, however, what was in fact arrhythmia inducing, were the guests standing beside Cleage. Detective Poole and her partner, Detective Miller, were gathered around Cleage. Miller glanced at his watch and Cleage shrugged. It looked like he had been doing a lot of shrugging.

Edgar ducked out of the doorway. *What to do what to do what to do.* This, indeed, was mad fuckery. Just what in Christ's name was going on? Police at his house? Detectives waiting for him in his classroom? The jig was up. He was caught. The heat had closed in. The devil doll stool pigeons had ratted him out.

Fuck it, Edgar decided, and walked quite calmly to the far end of the hallway to the small red-and-white box mounted on the wall. Edgar pulled the lever and the thin glass rod broke in half. Before the glass bits hit the floor, the fire alarm was blatting schoolwide.

Doors up and down the hall flew open, and students gushed out like water under pressure. From his distant vantage point, Edgar saw the detectives emerge among the students, Cleage right behind them. Poole handed Cleage a business card, and Cleage nodded his willingness to help.

Cleage and the detectives moved with the crowd—away from Edgar. Once they had disappeared out the exit door, Edgar moved forward with the thinning crowd. At his classroom, Edgar darted inside the empty room and found the blackmail note in his desk.

60

MAD FUCKERY

Back in the hallway, Edgar crossed to the boys' bathroom. He was going to rip the note into tiny pieces and flush it away. He didn't want it in his possession one second longer than necessary.

The bathroom wasn't empty. There were three stalls, a bank of sinks, and a row of urinals. Administration had taken the doors off the stalls some time ago to help curb the smoking problem. Jack Mendelson was standing just outside the first stall, and inside the privacy partition was everybody's favorite skinny Goth boy, Martin Kosinski. Two more boys, minions of Mendelson, were in the second stall together. Edgar heard the hiss of cigarettes hitting toilet water as he passed by them and ducked into the last stall. Edgar ignored them. Today was not the day to address this.

He did what he had come here to do, watching the bits of paper swirl away.

Head down, Edgar headed for the door. He heard Martin call his name, but, no, today was not the day. As the door slowly closed on its pneumatic hinges, Edgar heard Mendelson say, "Dude's a fuckin' coward," and then chortle in that special obnoxious way.

Edgar made it halfway down the hall before he turned back. As it turned out, today actually was the day.

Edgar walked purposefully back into the bathroom to find Mendelson casually going through Martin's wallet. He pointed at the two smokers.

"Didn't you hear the fire drill? Get out!"

The boys filed out, but Edgar grabbed Mendelson's arm to stop him from following.

"Do you want to make amends?"

"What? He was just showin' me his wallet. Look. Calfskin."

Edgar slapped the wallet out of Mendelson's hamhock hands.

"Do you want to make amends?"

"Dude, I don't know wha—"

Edgar slapped Mendelson. A hard crack, loud on the close tiled walls. The boy was stunned.

"Do you want to make amends?"

Jack Mendelson looked at Edgar and realized that something was very wrong with the world today. Mr. Woolrich had run amok. His glasses were cracked up like he'd been in a car wreck or something. Maybe he had been. He looked crazy. And that question, repeated over and over. It reminded him of the movie he'd seen where this crazy Nazi bastard tortured this guy with a dental drill, and he just kept asking the guy, "Is it safe?"

Then Mr. Woolrich slapped him again. Hard.

"Do you want to make amends?" *Is it safe?*

What was he supposed to say? What the fuck were amends? *Crack!*

"Do you want to make amends?" *Is it safe?*

Jack couldn't think. He needed to say something, but what? And then, Jesus, the crazy fuck hit him again. And Jack Mendelson, 220 pounds of brawn, found out he was still a boy deep inside. Tears sprang from his eyes.

"Do you want to make amends?"

"Yes. Yeah, sure. Whatever."

Edgar reached past Mendelson and pulled Martin forward.

"Martin, Jack wants to make amends. You want to make amends, right?"

Mendelson nodded uncertainly.

"Let Martin hit you."

"No fucking way. This is crazy."

"Oh, it's mad fuckery all right."

Edgar took Mendelson by the shoulders.

"Let Martin hit you. Trust me. Trust me on this. Look, see this gun?"

Edgar pulled Cornell's gun from his overcoat pocket. Both Martin and Mendelson recoiled. A firearm on school property was the single biggest sin that existed.

"This gun is yours," Edgar said to Mendelson. "I mean that two ways. Symbolically, and literally, since I'm prepared to say that I removed it from your person."

Edgar looked at Martin. The boy was cut into halves through his broken left prism.

"You'd back me up on that, wouldn't you, Martin?"

Martin nodded.

"A gun equals permanent vacation from school. Not to mention jail time. And maybe a nice cameo on the six o'clock news."

Edgar placed the gun in his palm and extended it to Jack.

"So, do you want this gun, or do you want to let Martin hit you?"

"He can hit me."

"Wise choice."

Edgar pocketed the weapon.

"I can see that your mind is very thorough. You are going to be so glad that this happened today. I'll tell you why. See, the horrible things you do to people, they eat at you."

Edgar paused and collected his thoughts.

"They eat at you, these horrible things you do. Especially later in life. They eat at you and you start to drink and take drugs to escape the memories. And then do you know what happens?"

Mendelson shook his head; no longer King Bully, but now just a scared kid.

"It's mad fuckery, that's what happens. You have to make amends to the people you've wronged. To stop the pain. Yours and theirs. So, I'm giving you this opportunity to make amends right now. This way, you won't kill someone's wife when you're out driving drunk one night."

Edgar motioned at Martin: *Get ready.*

"Martin, you have to do this. To save Jack. Promise me you will do this."

A change had come over Martin. He looked self-assured as he nodded in agreement.

"Good. Make amends."

Martin reared back, his fist poised like a cocked hammer. He hesitated only a moment, then realized that Mr. Woolrich was right. This needed to happen. He wanted it to happen.

The hammer came down and Jack's lip split open like an overripe plum.

Martin stared at his fist in disbelief—*Did I really do that?*

Jack's split lip spouted blood. He looked at himself in the mirror, and he too was in disbelief that this was really happening.

Martin examined his fist for a second longer, accepted the fact that yes, he had done that to Jack's lip. Then he slugged Jack three more times in rapid succession. *Bam-bam-bam.*

Jack turned and ran from the bathroom, hands covering his bleeding face.

Martin held his fist out to Edgar, showing him the dethroned king's blood smeared across his knuckles.

Edgar nodded, satisfied.

61

A FATE THAT LOOKED DARK INDEED

A calmness had settled over him.

Edgar had decided to let this thing play out however it was supposed to play out. He wouldn't evade it. Call it an acceptance of fate, but he no longer felt the feverish fear of the heat closing in. The devil doll stool pigeons could talk all they wanted. It was what it was. It will be whatever it will be. *Que sera* fucking *sera*.

The body was in the trunk, the gun was in his pocket, his wife was sitting next to him, and his daughter was asleep in the backseat. They were going home. All of them.

A mist from the heavy sky was falling over Mantissa Cove, and through the windshield, shadowy trickles of water crawled over Edgar and Helen's features. Edgar squinted at the road, his right eye blind, the left splitting the world in two.

The radio newscaster said a major nor'easter was likely to slam the area tonight, bringing with it the potential for storm surges, torrential rains, and hurricane force winds.

Edgar switched off the radio. Whatever tonight would bring, it was just a light mist on a gray day for now.

Not even enough to wash off the bloody thumbprint that adorned the trunk of Edgar's car.

They rode in silence, the unspoken pact still in effect. Don't ask, don't tell.

Helen turned around to check on her infant daughter in the backseat. Isabella slept, nestled in a rear-facing car seat.

Helen faced forward again. She stared straight ahead. At the oppressive gray day.

After a while, Helen turned to Edgar, opened her mouth, and her lips formed a question—but she stopped herself.

Edgar raised his eyebrows: *What?*

Helen shook her head gently—in resignation of questions best left unasked.

Edgar drove, moving forward into a fate that looked dark indeed.

62

CLOSING THE CASE

Detectives Poole and Miller stood next to their unmarked Crown Victoria in Edgar and Helen's driveway. Trench coats with upturned collars kept them dry.

Detective Poole smoked a cigarette.

Edgar saw them as soon as he pulled onto his street. He glided his car to a stop just above theirs.

Fate. Devil doll stool pigeons.

Helen squeezed Edgar's hand as he got out of the car. She turned around and unstrapped Isabella from the safety restraint. She held the baby to her bosom and pulled down the mirrored visor so she could watch Edgar and the detectives behind her.

Poole spoke first, no preamble.

"You've been missing. Two days."

"Did you check the hospital? That's where we've been. Had the baby."

"Know that now. Spoke with the principal at your school. He said you didn't call in. That it wasn't like you to just not show up. Said most likely your wife had gone into labor."

"He was right. In fact, I drove by the school to tell him in person, but they were having a fire drill. But yes, we had the baby. That's where we've been."

Poole looked over Edgar's shoulder, at Helen and the baby in the car, almost as if to verify this for herself. If Poole had shifted her gaze down just a bit, she would have noticed the thumb-shaped stain adorning the trunk lid of Edgar's otherwise spotless car.

But Edgar followed Poole's gaze, and he did notice it. And his heart sank. The thumbprint was holding on just fine despite the swirling mist. The moisture had renewed the color of it. It looked like what it was. Blood.

"You don't happen to know a man by the name of Cornell Smith, do you?"

Edgar looked puzzled.

"Can't say that I do."

"He's missing, that's all."

"Oh."

Edgar motioned to his car and said, "This is my daughter's first day home. What does this have to do with me?" Then he mentally chastised himself for drawing attention back to his car and the damnable telltale thumbprint. Mad fuckery, indeed.

Poole dropped her cigarette on the concrete driveway and

stepped on it. She looked up into the sky at the dark low-hanging clouds. A gust of wind pushed her hair back. She reached out and unexpectedly removed Edgar's cracked glasses from his face. She considered them, even held them out for her partner's inspection, but she never commented on them.

Edgar understood that Poole's invasion of his personal space was her cue to him that their relationship had shifted. That he was in a very serious predicament. That the heat had closed in.

She handed the glasses back to Edgar.

"See, that's funny. I would have thought, with me showing up at your home like this, I would have thought that you would figure that it must have something to do with your wife Judy's death. I mean, you used to show up at my desk every week asking if there was any news. Now I show up at your house asking do you know this man who's missing, and you don't even ask me if it has anything to do with your accident. That's funny. Don't you think that's funny, Alvin?"

"That's funny." Deadpan.

Lying was never something Edgar did well, especially when it required feigning ignorance, but he quickly shifted his facial features to something he hoped would convey sorrow and curiosity with just a hint of shame.

"Was he the one?"

"Was? Past tense. Don't know. But I do know this. His trailer burned to the ground two nights ago. His vehicle was there, but there wasn't a body recovered from the site."

There was a silence, and Edgar felt compelled to fill it.

"Could he be out of town?"

"Most people take their vehicles with them when they travel."

Edgar nodded.

Poole nodded back at him.

Edgar felt that enough time had elapsed that he could start to maneuver his body toward his car, to rest himself against the trunk. If Poole had seen the thumbprint, hopefully she would not see a cause and effect.

"I still don't understand why you drove out here to tell me this."

"Kind of a funny thing about Smith; he was arrested for shoplifting at the Walgreens right up the street from here. About eight months ago. His trailer is—excuse me, was—more than twenty miles from here. That's a long way to drive for a five-finger discount on a pack of Juicy Fruit and black hair dye."

He watched as Detective Poole extended her hand to her partner. Edgar took the opportunity to place his hand on the back of his car, striking, he hoped, a pose of idle rest.

Miller handed Poole a small plastic envelope with a piece of paper inside. A newspaper clipping.

"Even funnier thing. This was found in the glove compartment of Smith's car."

She handed Edgar the evidence envelope. The plastic sheath was beaded with moisture from the mist.

It contained the newspaper account of Edgar and Judy's accident.

"That clipping is over a year and a half old. But it was found in the glove compartment of Smith's car. Along with a slip of paper with your name and address written on it. Now that raises the question: Why would this missing man have an old news-paper clipping that concerns you in the glove compartment of his car?"

Detective Miller, speaking for only the second time, added, condemningly, Edgar thought, "Wasn't buried down deep, ei-ther. Was sitting right on top. Like he'd just looked at it."

"When you couldn't be found, there was some concern for your safety."

"That's right. And this Smith was a habitual drunk. Four DUIs."

"Four?"

Edgar glanced at Helen in the car. She had the baby in her lap, watching, waiting.

"Right. And he was a suspect in a hit-and-run case in Indi-ana seven years ago."

"Sounds like you've found the man responsible," Edgar said, handing the clipping back to Poole. He took the opportunity of movement to now lean himself against the back of the car. He used the seat of his pants to imperceptibly rub at the thumbprint.

Poole lit a fresh cigarette. The wind picked up and misty rain formed a nimbus around her.

"No. We haven't found him at all. The way I see it, it sounds like the man responsible is missing. And I've got a funny feel-ing that if he does turn up, he won't be breathing. What do you think?"

Edgar looked back at Helen and the baby, and this action was meant for Poole's benefit. "I think that would be just fine."

Poole arched her eyebrows and nodded.

"We had looked at him before all this. Looked hard. In fact, with the prior hit-and-run suspicion, the DUIs, we questioned him. Even had Science go over his car. Nothing. No physical evidence. No alibi either, so we never really cleared him."

Poole looked over at her partner, and Miller nodded in agreement.

"But I know you were running your own little private investigation for a while there. Your charts and graphs. And I was thinking that if we had looked at this Smith, maybe you looked too."

Poole crushed out her cigarette on the wet driveway.

"Maybe you took matters into your own hands."

Edgar shook his head. "I'm not that kind of man."

"Didn't figure you were. Just wanted to let you know what we found."

Edgar pushed himself off the back of his car, giving one last good rub with his ass. It seemed to be over. The heat had closed in and their loop had closed on nothing. Nothing at all. The devil doll stool pigeons had kept their mouths shut.

Doo-dee doo-doo doo-doo doo-doo; doo-dee dee-dee dee-dee dee-dee deeeeee.

The cell phone rang and the electronic notes of "The Entertainer" filled the air. *Goddamn it! Why hadn't he turned that damnable thing off when he'd had the chance?*

Edgar very nearly threw up on Detective Poole's black polished shoes. His legs did fail him, however, and he stumbled backward. Poole grabbed him.

"Easy."

Poole reached into her coat pocket, retrieved her cell phone, and answered it. "The Entertainer" stopped. She listened and nodded.

"Have you run the dentals? Give us five minutes."

She pocketed her phone.

"You okay?"

Embarrassed, Edgar said, "It's been . . . long. It's been . . ."

"Say no more. Go be with your family."

"Thank you."

"I'm closing the case. Your case. Figured this was as good a time to tell you as any. With your new baby, new wife, and all. It's over for me. What about you?"

"I'm satisfied."

Poole nodded and motioned Detective Miller into the Crown Vic. She sat in the car without closing the door and cranked the engine.

"Closed, that is, provided Mr. Smith doesn't turn up. In one way or another. At least, that's the way I see it."

"Yes. Me too."

"Good. So, what's her name?"

"Huh?"

"Your daughter, what's her name?"

"Oh. Isabella. It means—"

"Pledged to God."

"Something like that, yes."

"It's a beautiful name."

"Thank you."

Edgar turned to get back into his own car so he could pull it into the garage.

"Mr. Woolrich?"

Edgar turned back to the detective.

"Got something on the back of your pants there. Something red."

Edgar brushed at the bit of Cornell Smith's blood on the seat of his pants and watched the detectives back out of his driveway.

A NEVER-ENDING
SCHIZONUCLEOTIC NIGHTMARE

Jane and Steve peered down at the baby, cooing and making silly faces.

Edgar and Helen watched, proud.

"I know we should have waited a few days, but I just couldn't. She's beautiful, you guys."

"Thank you."

Tyler Ketchum came through the front door, struggling to carry a box of dinners that Jane had prepared for the new parents.

"Goddamn it, Tyler, I told you to put a plastic bag over the top. They're soaked."

Jane took the box and handed it to Edgar.

"Each one of these has a complete meal in it, okay? All you have to do is put it in the microwave. Ten minutes if it's frozen, five if it's thawed. You shouldn't have to cook for at least a week."

"Thank you, Jane."

"And we're gonna leave. Before the storm hits for real. Let you guys rest."

Kisses and hugs all around.

Day had given way to night, and the predicted storm indeed looked to be settling in. Edgar had thought that he would wait until the small hours of the morning, but it was dark now and the whipping rain would cover him nicely. He went to the garage.

Later, from the baby's room, Helen looked out the window over the backyard. Beads of moisture accumulated and trickled down the pane. She saw that Edgar had finished digging the hole. Now she watched him push a wheelbarrow across the backyard. From her vantage point, it looked like the wheelbarrow held a heavy, rolled-up rug. It would be even heavier, she thought, once the rain soaked it.

Helen sat down and fed Isabella. After that, she gave the baby a warm sponge bath and powdered her before wrapping her in a dry diaper. In the corner, Mitzi was sacked out, snoring like a cartoon, and nestled up to her warm belly were the fabled Yellow and Black Attack, Molly and Agnes. And seeing that, for some reason, made Helen believe that yes, everything was going to be all right. That life was good, and fair, and worth living.

When she looked out the window again, Edgar was tamping down the sodden earth with the back of the shovel blade. She could just barely make him out in the dark storm.

The sound of the rain was so constant that she almost didn't hear the doorbell. But she did hear it and went to see who would be bothering them at this most inopportune time.

When Helen saw that it was Martha, her fear was replaced with relief.

"I'm sorry for the other—"

Martha shushed her.

"All I want to know is if you're all right."

"I'm fine. We're fine."

"I thought maybe you'd started drinking again and Edgar was covering for you."

"No, nothing like that."

"He told me to fuck off. I almost shit my pants."

Helen laughed at that. And Martha did too.

"It's been a crazy week. We just got home from the hospital today."

"Oh dear, who was hurt?"

"Nobody. We had a baby."

"A baby! You had a baby?"

Helen nodded, grinning, and Martha squealed with genuine delight.

"Let me see that precious thing!"

* * *

Later, when Edgar peeked into the baby's room, Martha was standing over the bassinet, oohing and ahhing at the tiny new life.

"I'm sorry for the other—" Edgar began, but Martha waved him off.

"Water under the bridge. Your business is your business." She peered at Edgar. "You're soaking wet." Edgar was still wearing his shirt and tie—his Edgar suit—from the previous two days. He was wilted.

"Oh, I had to take Mitzi out for a walk."

"You might want to give some consideration to using an umbrella. Not that it's any of my business."

Martha plopped down in the sitting chair that matched the one Helen was resting in. She unshouldered her purse and placed it at her feet. She patted Helen's knee.

"I want for us to talk." Then, to Edgar, "Girl talk."

Edgar took off to his bedroom so that Helen and Martha could visit.

Martha leaned over with a grunting effort and began to rummage through her voluminous purse.

"I have something here . . ."

In the bedroom, Edgar congratulated himself on being able to interact with Martha in a normal manner. He unknotted his necktie, leaving the ends dangling down his chest. He stared at his reflection in the dresser mirror. He was surprised to find that he had no trouble looking himself in the eye. He felt good about himself, about the things he had done. Well, maybe *good* wasn't exactly right, not *le mot juste*, but he definitely didn't feel guilty. No, he did not feel guilty. Or did he? No, there was no guilt. Guilty people could not comfortably look into their own eyes in a mirror. And Edgar could look into his own eyes just fine. Just fine.

He didn't necessarily like what he saw in those eyes. A new depth was reflected in them. A new quality. It was knowledge, Edgar realized. He had been changed not by his own actions, but by the knowledge that he was capable of them. *What else are you capable of? Yes, Edgar, what other deeds might you commit?* And in looking into his own eyes, he saw that the answer was *almost anything.* He was capable of almost anything. He would protect his home and his family and himself from any and every outside threat. *But what if the threat came from the inside, old sport? From within you? What then?* Then he would deal with it. He would be vigilant. He would be watchful. He would be thorough. *Who had evaded the heat closing in? Edgar had, that's who.* Yes, he would be vigilant. Watchful.

And just what the fuck was that crafty-eyed bitch Martha doing here, this late, in the middle of a nor'easter?

"Really, Martha, it's not necessary. And that phone call the other day . . ."

Martha was still digging in her purse.

"Yes, that phone call. Had me worried. Did everything—"

"Everything turned out perfect. As you can see. Everything. Everything is perfect."

"You deserve it. You deserve everything that's coming to you. Truly you—wait, here it is."

Martha pulled out a clasp envelope and handed it to Helen.

"I really hate to do this, dear. I really do. And I probably should have waited for a better time, but . . ."

Helen opened the envelope.

There was a photograph inside.

And everything changed.

The photograph had been taken through a telephoto lens and showed Helen and Edgar ushering a bound Cornell Smith from his burning trailer.

"There's a whole series of these," Martha said. "It's like they tell a little story."

There was a humming in Helen's head, as though a high voltage switch had just been flipped, but her mind wasn't a sufficient transformer to handle the load. It was a synaptic overload. This was more than a human being could be expected to handle. The photograph slid from Helen's slack hands and landed faceup on the floor. A teardrop cut down her cheek. And her haunted eyes said what her mouth could not: *Life is* not *good, or fair, or even worth living. There is no escape. Life is just a nightmare.*

"It's what I do, dear. Sorry."

A never-ending schizonucleotic nightmare.

Helen looked up at Martha, but she was out of focus. Everything was out of focus. The only precise sensory input was the feeling of doom like a concrete wall. All was lost.

"You've known all along, right? This is what I do. I sponsor people. And they tell me their sins. Sin after sin after sin. They unburden themselves to me. It all works out in the end. Amends are made."

Helen shook her head, still unable to see. Her mouth opened to form a question, but she was likewise unable to speak.

"Oh yes. I work four different groups. You people are just so eager to get these nasty little things you do off your chests. Believe me, you're better off drinking. Well, maybe not you, dear."

Martha dug in her purse again and retrieved her car keys.

"Don't worry. It's not the end of the world. Really it's not. I'll call you and we'll work out the details. I'm sure we won't have to resort to breaking fingers or anything of that nature. Not with you. No, I think we'll be able to work out something quite reasonable. Pay as you go."

As her vision finally cleared, Helen could once again see her old AA sponsor. The permed white hair. The face Helen had once thought of as open and kind. Martha, the benevolent smart-ass. How had she let this happen? How could she have brought herself and Edgar all this way only to end like this?

"And again, I truly am sorry. But that's just the way I roll."

Edgar entered the room. "How, exactly, do you roll, Martha?"

Martha jingled the car keys in her hand. "I'll let Helen tell you later. I'd best motorvate."

Helen stood and went to Edgar. She grabbed him by the dangling ends of his loose necktie and pulled him down to her level. She brought his face to hers and kissed him. If there was hope to be had in this world, this was where she would find it. She yanked one side of the tie, and it slithered free of his shirt collar in a serpentine whisper.

Helen took the tie and in a single fluid motion wrapped it around Martha's throat. There was no time for Martha to react. No time for Edgar to react. She simply did it.

Martha grimaced. Gave out a short harsh grunt. Her face turned crimson. She looked like a woman who had just gone into cardiac arrest. Or perhaps had a major stroke.

Martha dropped the car keys, her fingers clawing at her neck. Helen stood behind her, gripping the ends of the necktie, twisting it tighter around Martha's throat.

Edgar's inertia broke. He took hold of Helen's hands, trying to break her grip, to peel back her fingers and wrest the tie free. Helen gave out an atavistic bark and motioned her head at the floor. Edgar looked and saw the photograph. He picked it up and although he could understand what he was seeing, he could not comprehend.

Martha bucked with life-or-death reflexes. It took everything Helen had to keep hold of her. She had to pivot her hips to drag Martha backward and keep her flailing limbs from overturning the bassinet.

Helen squeezed as tight as she could, her face showing nothing but grim determination.

Edgar watched, stunned.

As Martha fought her, Helen felt the concrete wall move back. Just a little.

Martha's movements grew even more extreme, even more

violent. Her fight for life was relentless, unexpectedly harsh, unexpectedly disturbing.

But finally her movements lessened. And this too was disturbing. Her life drained away. The two women crumpled to the floor.

Helen's concrete wall had dissipated. There was more than one cure for schizonucleosis.

She kept her grip steady, making sure.

Martha was still for what felt like a long time, but Helen wanted to be certain. Then a final seizure-like movement racked Martha's body.

And after a while, tiny involuntary tics were her only movement.

Until all movement ceased.

Still, Helen held on. She had to be sure.

Edgar reached out and touched Helen's arm.

And Helen let go.

She nodded at Edgar—as if to say, *Yes, you're right. My job is done.*

64

SOMETHING UNSPOKEN

Watching the storm through the baby's room window, Helen saw Edgar's reflection as he approached her from behind. He placed his hands around her waist and kissed her neck.

They looked into each other's reflected eyes for a moment, and something unspoken passed between them. Edgar left.

Helen continued to gaze out into the rainy darkness until cries from Isabella drew her attention away. She checked the infant's diaper and retrieved a fresh one.

Helen soothed the baby with a quiet lullaby as she changed her diaper. Singing softly, almost forlornly.

"Hush little baby, don't say a word, Mama's going to buy you a mockingbird . . ."

Helen sang the lullaby so softly, so slowly, it was almost a recital.

No, it was almost an elegy.

Behind Helen, through the window, Edgar trudged through the wet backyard.

Again, he had the wheelbarrow and shovel.

Edgar settled on a new spot at the far edge of their backyard and began to dig.

Helen finished changing her daughter. She scooped the baby into her arms.

Helen turned, holding the baby. They looked out the window together. At Edgar. Digging a hole in the rain.

Helen's voice grew even more forlorn now, even more elegiac.

"Mama's gonna buy you a diamond ring. And if that diamond ring turns brass . . ."

Even though it was not possible for her to hear it, the sound of the shovel penetrating the drenched ground seemed to accompany Helen's singing.

Her voice was so soft, so mournful, so out of place with the sickening harshness of the shovel striking earth.

Outside, Edgar looked up from his dark chore to see his wife and child silhouetted in the warm glow of the window.

He continued digging. And it seemed that Helen's funereal voice accompanied his task.

In the bedroom, the haunting lullaby was almost drowned out by the sound of the shovel violating earth.

"Mama's gonna buy you a looking glass. And if that looking glass gets broke . . ."

Mother and child watched Edgar, the husband-father-protector, dig Martha's grave.

At two thirty in the afternoon, while teaching his last class of the day, ninth-grade geometry teacher Edgar Woolrich reflected on the fact that—in what now seemed like another lifetime—his current wife, Helen Patrice-Woolrich, had successfully covered up the vehicular manslaughter of his first wife, Judy Woolrich. Helen had done this after a night of binge drinking and alcoholic blackout. She'd pulled it off perfectly. She'd gotten away with it. Except that she had forgotten that there was another witness to the crime. Someone else who knew what had happened.

Edgar further reflected that in addition to obstructing a police investigation, bringing a weapon onto school property, threatening a student with said weapon, and discovering that his current wife may or may not have killed his first wife—in

Grant Jerkins

addition to all that, Edgar and Helen had each recently murdered someone. One of these acts of homicide, Edgar's, could be construed to have been at least partly in self-defense and partly attributable to a species of situational rage, a temporary insanity, as it were (except, of course, for the prolonged period at the end when Edgar had tracked down—*stalked*, the word was *stalked*—Cornell like a wounded animal). The other killing, Helen's, had been committed, as the saying goes, in cold blood. No denying it. No gussying that one up with legalese. Lipstick would serve no purpose on that particular pig.

Edgar had no idea if this miasma of misdeeds, this cornucopia of crime, would continue to go undetected and unpunished. There were various witnesses to various acts. There was a vehicle that still needed to be disposed of (Martha hadn't walked there that night, had she?). DNA evidence that could never be entirely obliterated. Stories and alibis that didn't always make sense. There were dogs that were inclined to dig holes in backyards. Things of that nature.

The other night he'd used Martha's keys to get into her apartment. He'd found the photographs easily enough. And they did indeed tell a little story. A nasty little story. They weren't in 3-D, but they reminded Edgar of the View-Master reels he'd looked at as a kid.

There were no negatives, no additional hard copies, but he found the original high-resolution jpegs on the hard drive of Martha's computer. Most likely she'd only printed up the one photo. As an example. A hook. An attention-getter. Most likely. But who knew for sure? Edgar deleted the photos and emptied

290

the recycle bin, but your average reasonably bright high school student could recover recently deleted data files. It didn't take a computer forensics technician. Probably he should go back and retrieve the computer itself. Destroy it. Would the risks of doing that outweigh the perceived benefits? Perhaps Martha backed up all of her files with an online service. And she was almost certainly working with a partner (she'd been talking to someone about breaking fingers). The partner could have copies of the photonovel that was *Edgar and Helen's Excellent Adventure*. The partner likely knew Martha was planning a late-night visit to Chez Woolrich.

The question was not whether there were loose threads, inconsistencies, and evidence left behind, because there most certainly were. No, the real question was, would anyone ever care enough to even look? Because if someone looked hard enough, there was plenty to see. In fact, there was the ever-growing realization that he and Helen would never be completely free. Edgar knew that now. There would always be a dread sense of the heat closing in. There would always be the paranoid fear of the devil doll stool pigeons, eyes ablaze with feverish glee, hissing their names through yellowed teeth from behind closed doors.

No, trying to prefigure all of the possible outcomes would be like plotting irrational numbers on an infinite grid.

The lines of intersection were beyond reckoning, the variables endless.

God damn.